MW01125483

The Billionaire's Counterfeit Girlfriend

The Pryce Family Book One

nadia lee

For Jodi Henley.

Welcome to the Pryce Family series. If you've been following my Hearts on the Line series you've already been introduced to some members of the Pryce family.

When I first put Mark Pryce and Hilary Rosenberg into *Redemption in Love* (Hearts on the Line Book 3), I honestly didn't think they'd end up together. Mark was going to be Gavin's best friend, and Hilary was forever destined to be a minor secondary character. I didn't even give her any screen time until the second draft, and I sort of forgot about her until I started writing *Forever in Love* (Hearts on the Line Book 5). In a scene that was excised later, Hilary revealed that she dated only the most sedate, boring men.

That piqued my interest, of course. Why would a woman as intelligent and successful as Hilary do that? As I delved into her character, I realized that playboy *restaurateur* Mark Pryce was the perfect man for her, despite her protests to the contrary.

Those of you who've read *Redemption in Love* will get a chance to catch up with Gavin and Amandine. But if you're a new reader, you don't need to read any of the Hearts on the Line series in order to enjoy *The Billionaire's Counterfeit Girlfriend*.

I'll be releasing *Merry in Love* (Hearts on the Line Book 6) this winter, and afterward, I'll publish the rest of the Pryce family stories. I hope you enjoy getting to know them!

As always, I love and welcome reader feedback. Please email me at nadia@nadialee.net or connect via my blog (www.nadialee.net/blog), Twitter @nadialee, Facebook page (www.facebook.com/nadialeewrites) and group (www.nadialee.net/fb-group). I read and respond to all my emails and social media correspondence.

xoxo,

Nadia Lee

ONE

EXACTLY FOUR WEEKS BEFORE HIS FAMILY'S Fourth of July party, Mark Pryce walked into Omega Wealth Management. He'd tried to come up with a solution on his own, but the problem wouldn't go away. Only one person could bail him out of the mess he was in.

It was late, but he knew for a fact that Hilary Rosenberg rarely left at five.

A woman moved in his peripheral vision, and there she was. He turned to admire her. Unlike the other receptionists at the firm, Hilary was curvy, with generous breasts and hips that flared out in luscious slopes. She was dressed in a pastel mint-green blouse and cappuccino-colored pencil skirt that reached a single conservative inch below her knees. A simple updo revealed the kissable line of her neck. The only non-conservative item on her was a pair of sexy open-toe stilettos that improved the shape of her already gorgeous legs. He itched to reach out and touch her to see if she was as soft and sweet as he imagined, but he kept his hands to himself.

"Hi, Mark. You here to see Gavin?" Hilary walked past him to her desk. His body tightened at her delicious apple and cinnamon scent.

"Actually, I'm here to see you."

"I wish you'd called first. I'm leaving right now to meet some friends at Z." She dumped a thick stack of papers into her briefcase and picked up her purse and a gold-plated stainless steel travel mug etched with "A Woman Worth Her Weight in Gold." Her boss Gavin had given it to her a few years ago on her birthday, saying it described her perfectly.

Her brisk tone pricked his pride. Most women fawned over him. "It won't take long. We can talk in the elevator." He offered her his arm and almost chuckled when she predictably pretended not to see it. Well, no problem. If she didn't want to take his arm, he could do the next best thing—putting his hand at her elbow to guide her in a courtly gesture.

Generally, Hilary's interactions with Mark were limited to simple two- or three-minute conversations, mostly consisting of polite greetings. He was a playboy, and she didn't like playboys.

But she could see why other women succumbed to his charms. He was classically tall, dark and handsome with the clean profile his family was famous for. His blue eyes never failed to make her heart skip a beat, and his face often broke into a killer smile that was as lethal as a strychnine martini. Most importantly he wasn't some brain-dead idiot who'd inherited all his money. His father had given him a sizable trust fund, but he'd more than quadrupled its value with some wise investment decisions and a series of highly successful restaurants.

God must've been in a really good mood when Mark had been conceived. Grossly unfair, but such was life.

As they stood waiting for the elevator, she felt his gaze on her shoes and legs and did her best to ignore the warm sensation slowly spreading upward from her ankles. "So… What do you want to talk about?" she said, keeping her eyes on the elevator doors.

"I need a date for my family's Fourth of July party."

An interesting choice of topic. Mark was well aware it wasn't her job to provide him with dates. She sipped her coffee, taking her time…until he cleared his throat discreetly and rocked on the balls of his feet. She lowered the mug and took a deep breath. "Don't you have a girlfriend?"

"No. We broke up two months ago."

"What a shame." *Not.* Everyone knew Mark never dated anybody for more than three months.

"I know. That's why I'm asking you."

She choked on her coffee, and he pounded her lightly on the back. Wheezing, she drew away from him. "Are you *serious?*" she asked, looking into his eyes.

His gaze didn't waver. "Yes."

Why wasn't he laughing at her gullibility? Her skin prickled. A serious yes was not the right answer to her question. She turned away, looking straight ahead. "Surely you can find someone before the fourth." The mirror-like elevator doors reflected everything, and he made eye contact with her reflection. "You have a month," she said into her mug.

"I could, but 'someone' won't do. I need somebody Mom can't intimidate or manipulate to get to me."

"What's your mother trying to do?" Everyone also knew that Ceinlys Pryce wanted her children to marry into impeccable families.

"She's either giving my dates false hopes about marrying me or trying to get them to stay away." Even as his tone remained even, he rolled his shoulders. "I can't deal with that. Not all relationships were meant to go somewhere, and every time she tries to get them to leave me, they start clinging like scotch tape."

The elevator arrived—*finally!*—and they

stepped inside. Even with just the two of them, the interior seemed tiny today. She took a small step sideways to give herself more room. It didn't help. She could see their reflections again, this time on the inside of the doors—how his tall, strong body towered over her and made her feel somehow protected. Every time she drew a breath, the clean scent of soap and warm masculinity teased her. Her stomach fluttered like it was keeping hundreds of butterflies prisoner.

Her fingers tightened around her mug. "I'm afraid I can't help you." She kept her tone brisk. The key was to discourage him before he could work his charms. "I have a boyfriend."

"That doctor guy?"

"His name is Walt Goldstein, and he's a pediatric surgeon," she said, more sharply than she planned. Stable and staid, Walt was the perfect man for her. It'd taken years to find someone as wonderful as him, and no billionaire playboy was going to criticize him in her presence. "He saves babies' lives."

"He drives a Lexus with a license plate that reads BABYDOC." Mark's lips curled in the reflection. "Who gets a vanity plate with a Caribbean dictator's nickname?"

She tried not to scowl. "It's not like he's Haitian. Not everyone thinks of Duvalier when they see BABYDOC." She certainly hadn't…until now.

"Fine. Let's give him some credit and assume he really doesn't know any better. He still misses dinner an awful lot."

"And you track stuff like that."

"I avoid giving tables to people who don't show."

Apparently, she and Walt had canceled one too many reservations at Mark's restaurants. "I'm sorry," she said stiffly.

"It's not your fault. And I don't think he'll care if you go to some party with me on the fourth. There'll probably be a baby he has to operate on that day anyway."

She frowned. "Don't be mean."

"Oh come on, Hilary. There's something odd about a guy who keeps cancelling."

"Gavin," she said, referring to her super-busy boss—and Mark's best friend, "used to cancel his dates with his wife, but that didn't mean he doesn't love her."

Mark smiled. "And what has your doctor given you to make up for canceled dates? A private jet, perhaps? A yacht?"

"He's just doing his job."

"And I've helped you do yours. So you owe me."

Now that got her gaze swinging his way. "You have? I do?"

"Remember that special client luncheon you scheduled at Morrigan's? They screwed up the reservation, so I let you guys into the VIP area at La Mer at the last minute?"

He moved so that they were only inches away from each other, his body radiating an inviting heat. She always knew his eyes were blue, but not that they were the shade of the sunny Pacific. They beckoned her to say yes to whatever he was proposing because he was going to make it amazing for her. Her breath caught, and she couldn't speak through a hot lump in her throat. She should step away, but her legs felt like they were rooted in place.

"I bailed you out of a jam." He gave her that disarming grin. "It's time you do the same for me."

"Even if I wanted to, nobody would believe I'm your date." Her words tumbled out in a shaky whisper. She stole a glance at the floor number. Still only five. "I'm totally not your type."

"That's ridiculous."

"Is it?" She managed to tear her gaze from his and stared at the elevator doors—and their reflections. His eyes hooded, he studied her exposed neck like it was a piece of art…or his favorite dessert. Licking her lips, she took another gulp of coffee.

Hilary wanted to say no. She was afraid this wouldn't end well, but at the same time she did owe him one. He wouldn't have asked her if he weren't desperate, and she hated having unpaid debts. "If I do this, we're even. No more calling in favors."

"Of course not."

She took a deep breath. "Okay. I'll do it."

He grinned, and her heart thundered boom-boom-boom at being the sole focus of his smile. She could only imagine what it would be like if he decided to point all his formidable charm her way.

Thankfully, the elevator stopped with a gentle lurch, and they walked out together. As they crossed the first-floor lobby, the back of her neck prickled, and she shivered and looked around. There was nothing except polished marble, glass and chrome...plus uniformed security guards...a few sharply dressed people leaving work...and Mark.

For the past several days, Hilary had felt like she was being watched, which was ridiculous. Who would stalk her? She was too boring to stalk, and she'd cleared all the deviants out of her life more than ten years ago.

A twenty-something woman stood up from a backless leather seat and started walking toward them. She had pretty golden hair that curled around her soft, fair face. A pair of widely set blue eyes sat over a small nose and Cupid's-bow mouth that you normally only found on dolls. The pastel pink of her sundress further emphasized her youth and delicate beauty. Her gaze zeroed in on Hilary, and she snarled, "You bitch! You think you can steal my fiancé?"

"I'm sorry?" Hilary said.

"You should be! I was wondering about all those 'emergencies' Walt's been having recently, but guess what? When I called the hospital, they said he wasn't there!"

Hilary's mind blanked for a moment as she tried to process the situation, but her usually sharp brain refused to cooperate. She felt light-headed, like she was watching the scene happen in some faraway place to someone else who looked like her.

"Walt's your…fiancé?" This couldn't be real. It had to be some kind of sick joke.

The weight of several gazes pressed upon her, and she breathed deeply to clear her head. This was no time to panic.

"I found his texts and emails," the other woman was saying, looking Hilary up and down. "I can't believe it. What does he see in *you?*"

Hilary flinched. "Look I had no idea… I didn't know he was two-timing."

"Oh come on! He's a surgeon. Why wouldn't some overpriced coffeemaker like you want him?"

That snapped Hilary out of the mental fog. "Don't talk to me like that. I'm a victim here too." Walt had talked about proposing. Of course he'd never mentioned he already had a fiancée!

"Lying bitch! Why would he want somebody as fat as you? It's obvious what happened." She launched herself, and Hilary jumped back. She hadn't been in a fist-fight since her wild teenage years, and she certainly wasn't getting into one now in the lobby of her workplace.

The other woman shrieked when a pair of strong hands gripped her arms from behind. "Miss, calm down," Mark said.

"Let. Me. Go!" the other woman screeched, trying to twist around to face Mark. "This has nothing to do with you!"

"Yes, it does," he said. "The woman you're about to attack couldn't possibly have stolen your fiancé."

"How do you know?"

"Because she's my girlfriend."

The blonde stopped wriggling. "What?"

"I said, she's my girlfriend." Mark carefully let the woman go. "And let's face it; why would she want your fiancé when she has me?"

Hilary watched the blonde study him and the trappings of his wealth. Every item Mark was wearing cost more than what most people made in a week. Then there were his irresistible good looks. Walt was a nice enough looking guy, but nothing compared to Mark. "I don't know what you're trying to pull, but I saw emails," the blonde said, her voice considerably smaller and with less heat now. "They were meeting behind my back."

"You're making a scene. Walk away now unless you want me to have you thrown out."

"You can't do that!"

"Sure I can. This building is private property.

And you're trespassing." He gave her a blinding smile, then gestured to the security guards, who had been watching the show with their mouths open. They moved forward.

"If you or your thugs lay another finger on me, I'll sue!"

Hilary cringed. She didn't want Mark to get into trouble because of her. It was already bad enough he'd lied for her, and the situation was beyond hell-ish as it was. She stepped forward to stop the blonde, but he pulled her to his side for a tight hug. Hilary didn't even get a chance to react before he turned to the other woman. "Whatever you like. Leave your name with security so my lawyer can get in touch."

"I work for a law firm, you know!"

"Marvelous. Then you've heard of Rosenbaum, McCracken, Wagner and Associates. I'll have one of the partners call."

She paled at the mention of one of the top law firms in the state and finally turned and left, one of the security men following closely behind. Hilary winced at the name dropping, but if it ended the show...

Mark turned to Hilary, and his gaze softened. He tucked a wayward tendril behind her ear. "You all right?"

Unable to speak, she nodded and pulled away from him. Thankfully, he released her. She smoothed her hair with trembling fingers as she tried to process what had just happened. Had she just been confronted by her boyfriend's *fiancée?* Oh god. It was so obvious why Walt had promised to propose to Hilary.

She was an idiot with the worst judgment when it came to men, and they could tell by just looking at her. She was so naïve, she'd believe anything they said.

Just like her mom had gotten into trouble. Was it genetic?

There had to be something about her that broadcast how stupidly gullible she was. She'd chosen Walt with such careful consideration and thought. He was supposed to have been *the one*, her perfect man.

How could she have been so wrong?

"Hey, you look really pale. You need to sit down?" Mark said, laying a hand on her shoulder.

Aware of the audience, she forced a neutral tone and took a step back. Her mistake with Walt had blown up at work, but she wouldn't let it affect her career. "Thank you for your help. It probably would've gotten a lot uglier without you."

He smiled. "No problem. Sorry how it turned out."

"No, it's not your fault." It was all hers.

"So…about my family party—"

"What?" She clutched her stuff in front of her like a shield. "No!"

Then she ran out as fast as she could.

TWO

UMBFOUNDED, MARK STARED AFTER Hilary, who had somehow managed to sprint across the lobby in those shoes and vanished. What the hell was that about? Women never said no to Mark…especially after he'd heroically saved them. And getting rid of that psycho fiancée definitely counted as heroic. He'd even threatened to unleash the lawyers. Should he have threatened to do the same against Walt as well?

"Hello? Anybody home?"

Mark looked over to see his older brother walking toward him. "What are you doing here?"

"I saw you standing in here, staring at nothing like a fool. Since you didn't see me wave at you from the outside, I figured I'd come in and get you." Iain looked a lot like Mark—the height and the build were exactly the same—and they both shared the dark good looks of their parents. The only real difference was their eyes.

They walked out of the steel, glass and marble monument to power and money that was the Omega Wealth Management building. The sidewalks were thick with people striding purposefully by. Probably they all had somewhere to be, someone to be with…unlike Mark and his empty penthouse.

"You forgot about the party tonight, didn't you?" Iain said suddenly.

"No…"

"Good. It's gonna be a blast."

"…but I'm not going."

That brought Iain up short. "Why not?"

Mark shrugged. "What's the point? It's not like I'm going to find somebody who can keep my interest for more than a few weeks."

"Well if you don't go, for sure you never will."

"'Full of young, loose women and great booze' does not describe a setting conducive for finding that woman," Mark said, recalling their conversation that morning and tossing the two selling points for the party back at Iain. "If you want to go, go. You're old enough to not need a chaperon."

"Don't be a dick. I'm just trying to watch out for you and get you a date for the family party since your best friend won't."

Gavin Lloyd would never go out partying when he had the love of his life to go home to. Mark felt a slight ache at that. Jealousy? No. He was happy for his best friend. But he wished he could have the kind of relationship Gavin had.

Maybe it was *longing…*

"Okay, you need to stop with that look," Iain said.

"What look?"

"That weird look you've been getting ever since Gavin reconciled with his wife and his brother got married."

"It has nothing to do with them."

"Then is it Shane?" Iain said, referring to their youngest brother, newly set to marry his high school sweetheart.

Mark didn't respond. The snack he'd had earlier was sitting uncomfortably in his belly, but he was happy for all three of them. He was.

"Forget them," Iain said. "You have the kind of female companionship every man would kill for, going from one stunner to the next. Sure, the grass always looks greener on the other side, but it's not that green once you cross over. So what do you say to that party? Let's go!"

Mark shook his head.

"You can't go to the family picnic solo."

"Don't worry about that. I already found somebody."

Iain raised a skeptical eyebrow. "You did?"

"Yup."

"Who? Anybody I know?"

"Hilary Rosenberg."

Iain burst out laughing. "Get outta here."

"No, I'm serious."

"Hilary Rosenberg, as in Gavin's secretary Hilary Rosenberg?"

"She's his executive administrative assistant," Mark snapped. Didn't anybody know Gavin would rather fire half his analysts than Hilary?

Iain snorted. "Whatever. Stop joking around."

"Iain, read my lips. She and I are going together."

"But she's so…not your type."

Mark scowled. Hilary had said the same thing. "Okay, smart guy. What *is* my type?"

"Young blondes in their early twenties with tight asses and huge tits." Iain cupped his hands in front of his chest. "Fake or natural not an issue."

Mark's scowl deepened. He was pretty sure he'd dated some brunettes and redheads along the way.

"Mom's not going to believe you're dating her. She's going to set you up with that girl she wants you to marry. What was her name again? Katarina Luther or some such?"

"Yeah."

"I heard she's great marriage material," Iain said. "Just the kind of woman Grandmother would approve of. Mom's trying to marry all of us off, you know. I wouldn't be surprised if she has a list of candidates with my name written on them."

"Why is it so hard to believe that Hilary and I are an item?"

"If you are, then you'll pass the Inquisition, but you know how Mom is." Iain checked out a particularly leggy brunette walking past them. "She's going to grill both of you on things that all genuine couples would have done because she won't believe it's real. First date. First kiss. Presents. Likes and dislikes. It'll be worse than dealing with immigration."

"Immigration?"

"Yeah. A friend of mine married a girl from Vietnam, and to get the spouse visa they had to answer some really detailed questions to prove they didn't marry just to get her the visa."

Mark narrowed his eyes. Iain was probably right. He knew their mom better than anybody else.

"Hey, if you guys are really dating, fine. But I'm warning you if you're doing this to get out of her setting you up with Katarina."

Iain was right. Mark would have to do something to pass the motherly inquisition. No big deal. He would date Hilary for real for a month. She was a stunner, and she was single now. And most importantly, he liked her.

She'd probably said no because she was confused and hurt and angry at the male half of the population. Totally understandable, given the circumstances. She'd feel differently after a little wining and dining.

If not, he'd simply remind her she'd already said yes in the elevator. Given his experience with women and several months' worth of watching Hilary… How hard could it be to win her over?

HILARY STUMBLED ALONG THE CITY BLOCKS, PAST office buildings and the alleys that separated them. Some people turned away at the sight of her; others openly stared. The thick exhaust from cars filled her nose and mouth with grit and tears blurred her vision, but her feet moved forward like they knew exactly where she needed to go.

A Lexus pulled up next to her and honked. She turned toward it almost violently, thinking it might be Walt. Instead, it was her best friend Josephine Martinez. "Hey, girlie! Want a ride to Z?" Her voice was cheery as she lowered the window. Successful freelance personal shopper to the rich and famous, Jo was a stunner who dressed like a goddess. She took one look at Hilary's face, and the easy grin vanished. "Whoa. Okay, get in."

Hilary climbed into the luxury car. Jo placed a hand with purple-tipped fingers on her shoulder. "Are you all right? What happened?"

Hilary's lower lip trembled. "He's engaged."

"Who?"

"Walt."

"*What?*" Jo opened and closed her mouth a few times, then finally said, "Okay, start from the beginning. I'm totally lost." A car behind her honked, and she pulled into the traffic, rolling her eyes at the driver behind her.

Hilary drew in a shaky breath for courage, then told her friend a condensed version of the nightmarish scene in the lobby. Her stomach knotted so hard, it felt like her lunch would come back up. "How could I have not known that he's already engaged? It should've been obvious. I should've been able to see it."

"Nobody saw it. He was slick. I mean, *I* didn't even think he was a scumbag, and you know me."

"But—"

"He was always bailing on you, saying he needed to save a baby. Who could've known it was something else?" Jo plucked a tissue from a box she always kept in her car and offered it.

"Thanks." Hilary wiped her tears, then suddenly pounded a fist on her thigh. "Ah, I should've *known!* I should've been more *careful!* All my life, I've seen how men weasel into relationships. I saw how my mom and aunt ruined their lives over a worthless man, and I've had my share of jerks. There should be an asshole profile in the computer here."

She tapped her temple hard enough to make herself wince. "But somehow *I still pick them*. What are the odds of selecting a scumbag out of all the sweet baby-saving pediatric surgeons in the city?"

Jo patted Hilary's hand. "Not every doctor's noble, even if he's a baby doctor."

"You mean they aren't noble when I pick them." Hilary blew her nose. "I thought Walt was the one. He has everything—a good job, good education, an even temper…"

"A fiancée…"

"Yeah," Hilary said, sadness replacing her anger. "And a fiancée."

Jo squeezed Hilary's hand. "Don't be so hard on yourself. It's not your fault. He's the bad guy here."

Was he truly? Hilary tried to swallow through the hot lump stuck in her throat. She made a fist around the tissue, her hand shaky. What if this was his first time cheating on his fiancée? Maybe it was Hilary who had somehow inspired him to stray. Maybe he just knew… He could tell Hilary was the kind of woman men screwed on the side and had fun with, but wouldn't marry or do any of the respectable things that men did with undamaged goods.

At the next red light, Jo pulled out her phone and started typing rapidly.

"Who are you texting?" Hilary asked.

"Kim, so she knows we aren't going to be at Z."

"We're not?"

"We're going to my place. You're going to spend the night, vent all you want and get some sleep. Tomorrow, I'll help you get dressed. I'm going to make sure you look awesome."

"Does it matter?" Hilary worked for one of the richest and influential men in the world and dressed like a perfect administrative assistant. None of it made any difference. Her true nature might be too strong to cover up.

"Looking like a million bucks is the first step. You don't want to look pathetic over something like this. Don't worry, I'm not going to put you in anything sexy. Something tastefully gorgeous should do the trick."

"I don't know." All Hilary really wanted to do was crawl under a rock and play dead.

"You work for Gavin frickin' Lloyd. So you're going to dress like the woman who deserves to be the guardian of his inner sanctum. And trust me, nobody's going to feel anything except contempt for Walt. You just wait and see."

THREE

ILARY WALKED INTO THE OFFICE THE NEXT day in the outfit Jo had helped her select. Jo was right. Hilary still had to work there and face people. She'd rather not look like some pathetic loser right after the spectacle.

A fat *pathetic loser,* the voice of the blonde whispered.

Hilary's steps gained speed. At least her girls were real. That had to count for something, she thought, desperate to cling to anything even remotely positive about herself.

The security guards in their navy uniforms nodded as she walked past, scanning her security badge at the entrance. One of them was a substitute for the old-timer, Billy. She was sure Billy would hear about it the moment he returned.

Sally Smith was already at the main reception-ist's desk, the ever-present sleek bluetooth headset in her left ear. In her mid-twenties, she was short and pert, with Betty Page bangs and a small nose that made Hilary want to push it like a button. She was wearing a pale green and white dress that looked great on her stylishly toned body. Hilary had never seen Sally look less than fashionable.

"Good morning, Hilary." She gave Hilary a big grin and a broad wink. Huh. What was that about? Sally had no doubt heard about the incident from the day before, and she was too sweet to do anything except commiserate and offer support…except the grin and wink didn't. Hilary was certain there wasn't anything special going on that day, and she didn't know what could be making Sally react like that at the sight of her.

"Way to go, Hilary," said another administrative assistant, carrying a couple mugs of coffee to her station. Both of them were emblazoned with the unofficial company motto: a bright red "Short or Long—Who cares? I Win!"

Ooookay. This was just weird. What was going on? Was she getting some kind of secret bonus? A corner office? What was the deal?

Finally she reached her desk, which barred people from entering her boss's inner sanctum… and stopped short at the sight of a giant basket of pure ivory orchids and towering boxes of gourmet European chocolates.

There was a card at the bottom of the display.

"You gotta be kidding," she muttered. The extravagant present had to be Walt's attempt to get Hilary to return the bracelet he'd given her on their first anniversary a few weeks before. Encrusted with diamonds and pearls, it had no doubt cost him a fortune. She ripped the card from the package. Her anger subsided as she skimmed the message:

Remember—you said yes.
–Mark

She tucked the note back into the envelope and bit her lower lip. This was not what she'd expected when she'd walked out on him. Regardless, she hadn't been kidding when she'd said no in the lobby. Everything had changed when Walt turned out to be a two-timing bastard.

A few moments later, Gavin came in. Dark complexioned from his Italian heritage, he wasn't handsome the way Mark was, but his dynamic personality and intelligence made him stand out. He was in another of his crisp European suits, setting the standard for what everyone else at the firm wore. Outside of law firms, OWM was probably the only company in L.A. that had its workers routinely show up in suits.

A grin lit up his face. She'd noticed that he was smiling more often these days. "Good morning. Wow." He whistled. "Walt must've missed something big."

"It's from somebody else. Walt and I are through."

"Oh? Well, sorry to hear that." Gavin tilted his head, studying the gorgeous boxes of gourmet chocolate. "So who are these from?"

"A friend of yours, as a matter of fact. Mark Pryce."

His brow creased briefly. "Hmm."

"What?"

"Well. I'm just wondering… Are you two dating or something?"

She narrowed her eyes. What had Mark told her boss? "Why? Do you find it unbelievable that we might be dating?" Could her boss tell too that she wasn't the kind of woman men dated for real?

Gavin's gaze snapped to hers. "Unbelievable? No, it's just…"

"Yes?" *You're too fat and come from a totally fucked up family. The kind you see on trashy shows like Jerry Springer.*

"You know what his girlfriends are called, right?"

She folded her arms. "As a matter of fact, I don't."

Gavin pressed his lips together. Hilary frowned. This dithering wasn't like him. Finally he said, "Quarterly Girls."

"Quarterly Girls? What does that even mean?"

"He's never dated anyone for more than three months." Gavin shrugged uncomfortably. "And three months out of a year is…"

"Ah. The epithet fits."

"Yes." Gavin rubbed the back of his neck. "Don't get me wrong, he's a great guy. So it'll be fun while it lasts. But don't expect anything more. You understand what I'm saying?"

"Of course." She flashed him a quick smile, relieved he hadn't noticed what an enormous screw-up she was. "Don't worry. We aren't dating. I'm not even sure why he sent the stuff in the first place." He'd probably deluded himself into thinking that he could change her mind.

"Okay, I'll butt out." Gavin said, a frown still creasing his forehead. "You're smart, so I'm sure you know what you're doing."

MARK PULLED OUT HIS VIBRATING PHONE AS HE got out of his car in front of OWM. This was call number three from his mother, and he could put her off for only so long.

"Yes, Mother," he answered.

"What is the meaning of this?" came her low and furious voice.

"Uh… Can you be a bit more specific?"

"It's all over YouTube!"

"What is?"

"You and two women fighting like trailer trash at Gavin's company!"

Oh. That… Crap. "We weren't really fighting. I was trying to stop the woman from attacking Hilary."

"Hilary who?"

"Gavin's executive administrative assistant." Somebody should really come up with a cooler and shorter job title for Hilary. It was getting to be a mouthful.

She let out a soft gasp. "You got into a public brawl over some glorified donut fetcher?"

"Gavin doesn't eat donuts."

"Mark, I don't know the people who put the video up on YouTube. I can't ask them to pull it down without involving lawyers, which would only bring more attention to this…travesty."

"Then let it stay up there. Who cares?"

"If Katarina sees it—"

"Let her see it. She deserves to know what kind of person I am."

"But that's not you, Mark."

"Yeah, it is. No false advertising, Mom," he said, trying to leave the annoyance out of his tone. "Anyway I gotta go. Bye, love you." He hung up and shoved the phone into his pocket with a long, shuddering sigh. His mother had changed so much in the last twenty years or so, and it left a bitter taste in his mouth. The mother from his childhood wouldn't have been so set on playing matchmaker, or disapproved of all his ventures. Still, it was hard to be angry at her for being different now. She probably couldn't help how she was. She was the product of her marriage.

His parents might have been dubbed The Eternal Couple, but everyone who knew them even slightly knew that their marriage redefined the term *dysfunctional*. He couldn't remember a time when his father hadn't had a mistress, or when his mother wasn't pretending not to know about the woman du jour. Of course, there wasn't any point to her making a fuss about the situation. Thanks to the Pryce prenup she'd signed, she couldn't even force her husband to go to couple's counseling. And the agreement specified she would get nothing in case of divorce, regardless of who was at fault. Without love and respect, or the threat of being able to take her husband to the cleaner's, she was powerless in her marriage. And the powerlessness had become so overwhelming and toxic, it colored everything she did. He didn't understand why she hadn't left his father earlier, while she was still young and beautiful, to start over. He'd seen photos of her in her twenties. She'd been stunning. Hell, she'd been stunning into her thirties and forties as well. She could've had a fresh new life and found happiness.

Mark saw Hilary tapping away on her tablet inside the lobby. He glanced at his watch. It was just eleven forty-five.

There were women who could be devoured

in one bite, he thought as he opened the door and entered the building, but Hilary wasn't one of them. She had a zaftig allure that was out of a different era. Tall, with wide shoulders and hips, she had a waistline that somehow pulled everything together and skin so smooth the light shone off it. Today she was gorgeous in another pair of those sexy shoes and a conservative office outfit that consisted of a black sleeveless top and skirt. Her lips pulled together into a lovely pout as she concentrated on the tablet.

His fingers ached with the need to touch, but he sucked in a breath and mastered himself. He was too old and experienced to react like this.

"Hey," he said.

"Hi," she said without looking up.

"Let's have lunch."

"Sorry. I'm waiting for a friend."

"Forget that. Your friend can't get you what I can."

She tilted her head and looked up into his eyes. Her gaze was curiously blank. "You know, pursuing a woman who just broke up is never a good idea."

"I disagree."

"I'm really not interested."

"You said yes, remember?"

She swallowed. "That was before I was attacked in the lobby."

Was that a flash of panic in her eyes? Huh. "I don't see how that's relevant." When she opened her mouth, he raised a finger. "You owe me. Don't go back on your word."

"That was just for the party, not lunch." She scowled as a text from Jo appeared. *Sorry, can't make it. Stuck with a hysterical client on the phone.* "You know what? I'm really not that hungry, so I think I'll just go back to the office and get some more work done."

As soon as she said it, her stomach let out a loud growl. A man walking by actually glanced her way. Mark swallowed a laugh as Hilary's face turned bright red. "At least *part* of you seems to be hungry."

"Fine," she said in a clipped voice as she put her tablet away. "You can buy me lunch."

He chuckled. Ah the ever-gracious Hilary. He couldn't remember the last time he had this much fun with a woman. "Did you like the flowers and chocolate?"

"Yes. Thank you. They caught me by surprise. I thought they were from Walt."

"Please." Mark shook his head, put a hand on the small of her back and gently guided her outside. "I'm pretty sure he's never given you anything that extravagant." That cheapskate doctor had never ordered the best wine on dates at Mark's restaurants. Why? Because the best cost the most. Everything at the restaurants was superb, but if Mark had been dating Hilary? He'd get her only the finest because that was what she deserved.

Until the three-month mark, right?

The small muscle in his jaw jerked at the nasty reminder. Hilary walked next to him, and her skin glowed in the bright Los Angeles sun, her hair gleaming fire and her scent making his mouth water. He'd been fantasizing about licking and kissing the amazing slope of her neck since the day before. Beautiful women were a dime a dozen in L.A., but none of them drew him the way she did. She never let him get away with anything, and she was sharp and hard-working. Would he really get tired of her after three months?

Jesus. What the hell was wrong with him?

Thankfully, Hilary distracted him by saying, "I thought he was trying to get me to return his bracelet."

"Keep it or pawn it," Mark said roughly. "You shouldn't have to give it back because he's a two-timing jerk."

"You're probably right."

"Hop in the car," he said, opening the door to his Bugatti. "And let's go."

"Where?"

"You'll see." He drove, weaving in and out of the early lunch traffic. "Just so you know, somebody put the scene at the lobby from yesterday up on YouTube."

She covered her face. "Oh no."

"Don't worry about it."

"How did you find out?"

"Mom saw it."

"Oh my god. She and how many other people?"

He shrugged. "Who cares? Most of them are strangers anyway, and the person who should be ashamed of himself is Walt."

Dropping her hands, she looked outside and sighed. After a few moments, she asked, "Why lunch?"

Several flippant responses leapt to mind, but he chose honesty. "I need to make people think we're a real couple before the party." He gave her a quick grin. "So sit back and enjoy the courtship phase, where I'm trying to get to know everything about you."

She laughed, the sound reluctant and repressed at first, then growing more free-flowing as she shook her head. Was there an odd undertone of disbelief and semi-horror? Maybe he'd imagined it. "What's there to know?" she said. "I'm a pretty boring person."

"I don't think so." A boring woman wouldn't have had the confidence to stand tall and proud, despite the ample curves that had somehow become unfashionable in the last few decades. A boring woman wouldn't have the brainpower or emotional control to manage the schedule of somebody as dynamic and busy as Gavin. And a boring woman definitely wouldn't have possessed the silent siren allure that seemed to be all Hilary's own. Mark found her irresistible.

He pulled into an empty parking lot; before them was a semi-gutted building. "Come on," he said, opening the door for her.

She stepped out and stared at the dark and barren place. One of the big front windows was missing; the other still had white tape crossing it diagonally. Some of the girders were exposed, and loose wires hung from the ceiling like vines in a jungle. "Wow. This is sort of unusual. Most people go to restaurants or a food court."

"Yeah, I know." He cleared his throat. "The place is nowhere near ready yet, but the chef wants to show off some stuff. I figured I'd bring you."

"This is going to be another one of your restaurants?"

"That's the plan. French-Japanese fusion."

"What's the name of the place?"

"I haven't decided yet. But inspiration will come. It always does."

"I thought you were going to start a new restaurant in Houston."

He gave her a crooked smile. There was one benefit to her working for Gavin: she heard about him. Now he just needed to make her more aware of him as a man. "I've been looking into some possibilities there, but I haven't found anything that really catches my imagination."

She started toward the building, intrigued despite herself. "When are you going to open it?"

"When it's ready." He gently took hold of her wrist, resting his thumb over the pulse point. He could feel it throb against his bare skin, and his heartbeat picked up its pace to match hers. His breath caught. How could this simple touch make him feel like he was fundamentally and inexorably connected to her? He found that he didn't want to let go. "Come on. Our lunch awaits."

FOUR

T HE INTERIOR WAS STARK. THE WALLS NEEDED paint; the floor something other than the flat concrete surface. Panels of drywall were stacked in a corner, a circular saw lying on them with its cord hanging over the edge. The only section that seemed complete was the bar in the front—but then Mark *was* an expert bartender—and an open kitchen with state-of-the-art appliances and gas stoves and grills and everything else a chef could possibly want. Curved track lights lit the counter like a stage, and a stout, dark-haired man—probably the chef for the new restaurant—nodded at them.

"What do you think?" Mark said.

"I like the bar," Hilary said.

He laughed. "Who cares about the bar?"

"You, apparently." As she got close, she could make out intricate patterns on the counter that looked Asian. She didn't know eastern art well enough to know if it was authentically Japanese, but she knew Mark didn't believe in neglecting details. "So what kind of design theme are you thinking of?"

"Clean. Minimalist. Lots of open space, but with a sense of privacy for the diners with strategic screens and translucent silk hangings. They're going to be embroidered by hand, and each is going to be unique. I already have an artist who's working on the designs." His eyes bright, he gestured at the loft. "That up there is going to be turned into a special seating area for parties or business dinners or whatever. When people come in here, I want them to feel like they're on a pleasure boat with the most incredible culinary delights. I'm also in the middle of formulating my own specialty cocktail recipes for the restaurant."

She had no idea how he was going to merge French and Japanese aesthetics, but if anybody could do it, it was him. People had thought he was crazy when he'd explained his ideas for La Mer. It would be surrounded by walls made of aquariums and serve the best seafood in the world. It'd turned out to be one of the most successful restaurants in the country. Everyone talked about it, and everyone wanted to go there. "I can see how this place could become something amazing."

He grinned. "You think so?"

"Yes." She grinned back. "I hope you let me in on opening night."

"You got it. A VIP table and the best champagne, on the house." He pulled out a chair at the only table that had a cloth over it. "Please."

After she settled in, he sat down and draped a thick cloth napkin over his lap. "You have to tell me honestly what you think about everything."

"I can try, but I do need to go back in an hour or so."

"Gavin can tie his shoes without you for a little while."

She chuckled. "People give me entirely too much credit." Still she couldn't deny a small pleasure at hearing Mark praise her professional capacity. It was important—the only thing she could count on, really. No matter what anybody said, people didn't stay the same. They changed…generally for the worse…and let her down.

A server she remembered seeing at La Mer brought out a small appetizer of green crepes made with avocado, cream cheese and smoked salmon. A giant raw shrimp joined the plate, its succulent body bathed in light, lemony sauce. "This is really good," she said after a bite.

"Think so?"

"Uh-huh. Where did you find the chef?"

He popped a small piece of crepe in his mouth and nodded with approval. "I met him in Marseilles."

"French?"

"Well, ah, yes…"

Okay, that had sounded dumb. She resolved to do better. "How did you get him to come over?"

"He said he wanted to work at a place where his talent was appreciated. Apparently he thought I appreciated his talent the most."

"You like his food."

"Yes. There's nothing to really nitpick. He's one of the most brilliant *cuisiniers* I know"—Mark leaned across the table and brushed the back of her hand gently—"although you shouldn't tell him that. His head might get too big for that chef's hat."

She chortled to hide her reaction to his touch and reached for her glass. She didn't know why his barest stroke made her want to take his hand in hers. "All right. I'll keep that in mind."

The rest of the lunch was excellent, but not quite as leisurely as she would've liked since she had to go back to work. The entrée was sea bream in the most delightful butter sauce with the barest hint of wasabi. Somehow they worked beautifully together to compliment the firm, fleshy fillet. The final course consisted of slivers of hard cheese, fresh berries and crème brûlée.

"Mmm, my favorite," she said, taking a big bite.

"I don't know anybody who doesn't like crème brûlée."

"Too bad. I'd help them finish their dessert." The top was caramelized to perfection, the sugary film extra sweet and crisp. She sighed with pleasure. "Do you know how to cook?" She was always curious about that.

"Me?" He blinked like the notion was somehow unthinkable. "No."

"Not even the most basic stuff?"

"Nope."

"But you own so many restaurants."

"Exactly. I own them. I don't cook in them. If I did the places would go bankrupt." He flashed a quick grin. "But I'm good at making drinks. So when a new restaurant opens, I might bartend for a few weeks to see how things go. And to say hi to people who come by."

Mark had lots of friends, most of them well-connected and wealthy. Mark's restaurant menus didn't have prices on them. If you had to ask, you couldn't afford the meal.

Unless you were one of his Quarterly Girls.

"What?" Mark said.

"Huh?"

"You had an odd look just now. What is it?"

Surprised at his observation, she took a sip of her ginger ale to give herself time. "Well. I was just thinking about your reputation."

"Ah." He leaned closer and gave her a wicked smile. "The whole awesome lover thing? I have to tell you, it's entirely deserved."

"Not that." She felt her cheeks heat like a young

girl's. What about him made her smile so easily and blush? It was like she was back in her teenage groupie years or something.

"You know—"

Her phone beeped, and she almost jumped. "Sorry." She held up a finger. "Let me just check that." It was a reminder about the big banquet for a charitable foundation Gavin was involved in. She needed to follow up on a few details and have a conference call with the organizers to finalize everything. With Gavin's wife Amandine still without an assistant, Hilary was taking on more work to smooth things out with their philanthropy projects. "Oh shoot. I'm sorry, but I really do have to get back to the office."

"No problem."

As she stood up, he took her hand. The touch sent shivers along her arm, followed by heat unfurling in her belly. She swallowed. Good god, this was dangerous. She shouldn't be attracted to somebody as bad for her as Mark would be. She started to pull away until she noticed his disarming smile. This contact meant nothing to him—it was something he did because he was Mark. It'd be ludicrous for her to make a big deal about it.

"Thank you for the lovely company, Hilary. I enjoyed it very much."

"Me too. And the food was amazing."

"So," he said, eyebrows raised expectantly, "about our next *rendezvous* before the party…"

The man was relentless…even if he did have a pretty good French accent. "Why do you need a date to this party? It's just a family thing, right?"

He looked at her for a moment, then said, "If I show up solo, I'm going to be set up with a woman my mother deems perfect for me."

"So?" Maybe his mother knew just the type of woman her son wouldn't dump after three months.

"I'm not interested. I'm not the kind of guy who does commitment."

Hilary laughed. "It's just a little set-up, not a marriage." When he didn't laugh, she peered at him. "Isn't it?"

He shook his head grimly. "I'm pretty sure they're picking out china even as we speak."

She pulled her lips in. She didn't want to help him out. Associating with a playboy who threw her off her equilibrium was equivalent to standing next to a ticking time bomb and hoping it wouldn't go off. On the other hand, she owed him one, and he was asking for a relatively simple favor. "Fine. I said I'd go. You don't have to take me out for the entire month."

"Oh no, we do." He gave her the most wicked grin. "Remember—we have to make everyone think we're a real couple."

Around seven thirty, Hilary pulled into the driveway of her aunt's humble two-story home in a lower middle-class neighborhood that once had been nicer but now had a run-down feel. The houses had a mildly worn look about them, reflecting their owners' priorities. Most didn't have the time or money to garden or paint or do any fancy upkeep. But none of them looked grossly neglected either.

She frowned when she saw a shiny black Mercedes in front of her aunt's house. No one in the neighborhood owned a car that expensive, and she doubted her aunt knew anybody rich enough to drive one.

As she got out of her environmentally correct Prius, the Mercedes flashed its high beams at her. She raised a hand and squinted. There was a man behind the wheel, but he didn't look like anyone she knew.

He got out, wearing a chauffeur's uniform, and opened the back door. The familiar figure of Ceinlys Pryce unfolded from the car. She was still a gorgeous woman, apparently having taken good care of herself in the last few decades. From what Hilary had heard, Ceinlys had been one of the greatest beauties of her generation, which was how she'd managed to snare Salazar into marriage. Her high society husband had a reputation as the biggest player around, with probably at least one mistress in every major city in America, and maybe Europe as well.

A dress as black as her hair added severity to her solemn expression. There was a ruby brooch on one slim shoulder that glittered like fresh blood. Stylish high heels with diamond accents encased her small feet. Everything about her was expensive and elegant. "Hilary," she said. "Mind if we go for a drive?"

The invitation didn't sound all that friendly. Not that her voice was frosty or rude. Far from it. It was the aloof way she held herself and spoke.

On the other hand, what could Ceinlys do to Hilary? Maybe she was just concerned about the unfortunate video on YouTube. "Sure."

Ceinlys disappeared into the car, and Hilary followed. The driver closed the door and started pulling away. Ceinlys raised the partition. "I heard about what's going on between you and my son."

"I'm sorry about the incident in the lobby."

"I beg your pardon?"

"I heard that you saw it on YouTube."

"Ah that. Yes. It was quite...vulgar, but somewhat to be expected. But I'm not here to talk about that."

It was Hilary's turn to be surprised. "You're not?"

"I'm wondering what you're doing with my son. I heard you had lunch with him."

"Wow, news travels fast. Are you having him watched?"

Ceinlys went on like Hilary hadn't spoken. "He might be a younger son without the responsibility of carrying on the family legacy, but he's still beyond you, my child. I don't want to see you get hurt."

"I appreciate your concern."

"Do you?" Ceinlys tilted her head and regarded Hilary with narrowed eyes.

"I understand what you're trying to tell me, and I already know enough about your son's past."

"Many a woman has tried to change him."

"So I've heard. But I won't."

"Are you saying Mark's not good enough for you?"

"I'm saying we aren't compatible." That hadn't stopped Hilary from agreeing to help him out, but she wasn't going to tell that to his mother.

Ceinlys considered. "You're serious."

"Why wouldn't I be?"

"He's worth a couple of billion at least."

If anybody thought a man's money could persuade Hilary, they needed to think again. "I'm surrounded by wealthy men, ma'am. I'm not so easily dazzled by it."

The older woman laughed, the sound oddly brittle. "Ah yes, I forgot. You work for Gavin, who likes to flaunt his money."

"He does?"

"The jets, the yachts… All quite vulgar. If that isn't flaunting, what is it?"

"Caring for his wife isn't flaunting."

The good humor fled Ceinlys's face, and she grimaced as though she'd just bitten into a rotten fish. "Perhaps."

Before Hilary could ponder that, Ceinlys's expression returned to its former cool politeness. She lowered the partition. "We're finished," she told her driver and raised it back up. Settling into her seat, she stared serenely ahead.

Hilary stole a few glances at Ceinlys. She seemed so aloof, Hilary wondered what kind of woman Ceinlys had in mind for Mark. Probably somebody just as distant and expensive as herself. Poor Mark. His actions made more sense now.

The driver took a few more turns before pulling in behind Hilary's car. As Hilary climbed out of the Mercedes, Ceinlys murmured, "I'm glad we had this talk and understand each other, my dear. I'm sure we'll get along quite well."

The door shut, and the car sped off before Hilary could think of a suitable response.

HILARY UNLOCKED THE DOOR AND WENT INSIDE the house, dropping her purse on the half-sagging couch. The carpet was older than Hilary, and the interior hadn't been painted in years. She wanted to replace the carpet and freshen up the walls, but her aunt had refused. "Waste of money, my dear. You don't want to stand out in this kind of neighborhood."

Maybe so, but they didn't have to live so poorly either.

Her aunt came out immediately. She was in a flowery house dress that reached an inch below the midpoint of her shins. In her late fifties, Lila was short and skinny. She'd lost weight after Hilary's mother's death. It worried Hilary, but there didn't seem to be any way to make her eat like she was supposed to. Lila had insisted she no longer had any appetite. Still, she made an effort when Hilary came home.

"Who was that?" Lila asked.

"Oh. Just somebody I know through work." Which was sort of true since Hilary had first heard about Ceinlys after she'd started working for Gavin.

"What a beautiful woman. Was that her husband driving?"

Hilary laughed at the idea. Ceinlys would never have married that poorly. "It was her chauffeur."

"My goodness." Lila clasped her hands on her wrinkled and sunken cheeks. "Her husband must treat her like a princess."

If unfaithfulness was part of the royal treatment package. "Depends on how you look at it."

"Lucky her." Lila sighed. "It reminds me of how Tim used to love me. He made me feel like the most beautiful fairytale princess. You know…Cinderella."

If Prince Charming had treated his lady love the way Tim had treated his, the story would've been beyond tragic. "Tim was no prince," Hilary said, unable to help herself.

"Don't speak like that about your father."

"He's also Bebe's father." Bebe was Hilary's cousin, and Lila's daughter. "Never really knew what to call him. Dad? Uncle Tim?"

"All the more reason to show some respect, young lady."

"Are you kidding? He got you and Mom pregnant *on the same night*, given that both of you went into labor one after the other and delivered us within thirty minutes of each other."

"It was only a few minutes apart," Lila said testily.

From what Hilary had pieced together, the birthing had been some kind of competition—who would have Tim's baby first. Hilary's mom had won, but Lila insisted it was the paperwork mix up at the hospital that robbed her of the joy of giving Tim his first child.

Hilary didn't think it was something worth worrying about, especially out loud. If it had been her in that situation, she would've kept her mouth shut out of mortification. But it had been one of many contentious issues in her mother's and Lila's relationship.

All because of a stupid worthless man that neither woman had been able to give up.

Tim hadn't cared about his children any more than he had about their mothers. He'd run off once he'd decided he didn't enjoy changing diapers. He'd come back after Hilary and Bebe were three only because he'd run out of money and his hooker girlfriend kicked him out for smoking crack in front of her boy.

Hilary stared at her aunt, then thought of her wild cousin who'd left to do god only knew what. None of the Rosenberg women had turned out well…except Hilary. No. Not even her. Just look at how Walt had been using her, just like Tim had used her mother.

Hilary rubbed her temples, suddenly tired. "Never mind, I'm going to bed."

"Without your dinner? I made quesadillas."

"I already had some Chinese," she lied, her appetite gone.

FIVE

ARK SENT ANOTHER EXTRAVAGANT BAS-
ket of flowers and chocolate. Since there
was no way Hilary could eat that much
chocolate, she shared it with everyone, much to
their delight.

The entire office didn't need to know he was
interested in her, especially when it was simply a
ruse and would end in one month. Still, a part of
her thrilled at the attention. It was sweet that he
bothered.

As she was going over Gavin's latest itinerary,
her cell phone buzzed. She checked the message. It
was from Mark.

*We're going to a charity event this weekend to
raise money for some foundation my cousin likes.*

She quickly wrote: *I have other plans.*

A few seconds later, the phone buzzed again.

Don't you want to feed the hungry? And not just any hungry, but children! Think of the children!

Despite herself, she felt her lips curve into a wry grin. *Are you trying to guilt me into going?*

Depends. Is it working?

No.

Aren't you bored? What else are you doing? Say you'll come. It'll be awesome.

She pressed her lips, but they curved in a smile anyway. *Fine. Send me the deets.*

Putting the phone on the desk, she tried to focus on the morning's tasks. As unwanted as the situation with Mark was, at the same time it was an excellent rebound charade. If it hadn't been for Mark's rather blatant interest so soon after the fiasco in the lobby, she would've become the office's object of pity for a while. There was something sad and pathetic about a woman who got attacked by her boyfriend's fiancée in the office lobby.

Hilary didn't do sad and pathetic. She'd rather die first.

After a few hours of getting everything squared away, she checked her emails and frowned when she saw one from Kimberly Sanford, Salazar Pryce's administrative assistant.

Can we meet for lunch? It's sort of urgent. My treat. I need to pick your brain.

Hilary frowned. She and Kim were pretty

close—Hilary was something of a mentor to Kim, who was in her early twenties—and this sounded semi-serious. *Don't need to pay for my lunch, sweetie,* she typed. *Meet me at Galore at noon?* Galore was a small sandwich shop about halfway between Gavin's and Salazar's offices.

A few minutes later, a reply came: *Yes. Thank you so much!*

At a quarter till, Hilary checked in with Gavin to make sure he didn't need anything else from her, then left for Galore.

It was owned by a Chinese couple—or at least Hilary thought they were Chinese—who made the most amazing sandwiches. The décor was simple with studio lights, dark faux-wood tables and chairs. The moment she walked in, she was in heaven. The warm scent of freshly baked bread and gurgling coffee beckoned. Sweet melodies by Norah Jones came softly from the sound system.

"Long time no see, Hilary," the owner said behind the counter. Friendly and earnest, he was about medium-height and had coarse, straight jet black hair cropped short. Old grease stains marked the white apron he wore over his T-shirt and shorts.

"Hi there, Min." She ordered her favorite—a BLT with apple-smoked bacon, organic tomatoes and lettuce, and a side of small fries. Yum.

"Iced latte?" Min asked.

"Yes, please." She took her tray and took the last available table near the window. Soon after, Kim joined her with a BLT.

Kim was a stunning brunette with a tall model's body and pouty sexy lips that were in fashion. Unlike a lot of women in L.A., hers were completely natural. She wore a well-fitted red dress and a cute black dress jacket. Her face, with large green eyes and soaring cheekbones, would've been flawless if it weren't for the thin white scar that started near her left ear and stretched all the way down to her mid-jaw. She always wore her hair in long parentheses to cover the jagged imperfection as much as possible.

"Thanks for seeing me on such short notice," Kim said.

"No problem."

"How are you holding up by the way?"

"Oh." Hilary shrugged. "I'm all right, now that the shock's worn off." She cleared her throat, uncomfortable talking about the mess Walt had made. "What's up?" She bit into her sandwich. It was amazing, especially with the smooth taste of the house specialty mayonnaise. Nobody knew what the cook put in there, but it was cracktastically good.

"Salazar's quitting."

"Huh?"

"He's retiring. He told me so today." Kim lowered her voice, sipping her latte and looking like she needed something stronger. "Please don't tell anybody. Not even his wife knows yet."

Hilary waved a ketchup-laden fry around. "What's going to happen to the family business?"

"Dane's probably coming back to take over."

"Oh." Dane was the oldest of Salazar's children. "And…he's bringing his own assistant?"

"That's my understanding."

"Ah, that sucks. I'm sorry to hear it."

"Yeah. So I'll be job-hunting soon. I'm hoping that having been Salazar's assistant might help me land a new gig."

"It'll definitely help. You've been with him for two years. Nobody else's lasted as long as you have." Salazar always hired the best looking executive administrative assistants he could, then had affairs with them *after* he'd fired them. Hilary had heard that it was to prevent sexual harassment lawsuits. But he hadn't done that to Kim—and it wasn't because she was ugly. Kim was gorgeous, and her boss basically hit on anything that lacked a Y chromosome. Hilary was certain he'd hired Kim precisely because of her youth and beauty, but kept her because she was so good at her job it actually outweighed the sexual considerations.

Of course, that was the sort of recommendation that was hard to put on a résumé.

"The job market's awful right now, you know,"

Kim said, her voice glum. "I just bought a new car and moved into a bigger and better place. My old place was a dump."

"Has Salazar said anything about your future at the company? Maybe he can use you in some other capacity."

"I don't think so. I'm so scared, Hilary. It took me months to land this gig. I thought I was secure after two years. I did everything right."

"I know." Hilary patted Kim's hand. "My real worry isn't even your losing your job, but what Salazar might do. He might try to make a move on you, since you won't be working for him anymore." Hilary didn't want that for Kim. Men like Salazar were predators, who used up women like Kleenex. Crap like that could change a woman, even a strong one like Kim. Despite his age, Salazar was still handsome, charming and could be extremely persuasive when he wanted. "Look, send me your updated résumé and I'll see what I can do, okay? But meanwhile, don't panic and most importantly, do your job. You don't want to screw this up. It'll work out, I promise. Also I can put out some feelers for you."

"Thanks." Kim forced a wan smile. "I can't believe this—me, running to you over every little crisis."

"Hey, that's what mentors and friends are for." Hilary genuinely liked Kim. She could've cruised through life trading on her good looks, but she didn't. It was like the idea had never even crossed her mind. Unlike certain women, she hadn't applied to work for Salazar because she'd aspired to be his new wife. In close to forty years, no one had been able to replace Ceinlys, and Hilary doubted anyone could.

"I would've never kept my job this long without your help."

"Don't give me too much credit. You're the one who went to work every day and did the job. I just offered some pointers."

"I can't believe how lucky I was to meet you at Salazar's luncheon. You saved my bacon there."

Hilary laughed. "Oh my gosh, you still remember that?"

"How could I forget?"

They'd met at a business luncheon that Salazar had decided to host. Gavin had been invited, of course, and Hilary had accompanied him with some critical documents. The event had been planned by the previous assistant—who'd been fired within two months—and a lot of details hadn't been set right. Kim had been close to tears, and Hilary had told her exactly what to do. She'd expected Kim to get even more hysterical at the idea of having to fix the mess—most of the pretty young things Salazar hired were pretty useless for anything except painting their nails, but Kim had pulled herself together and taken charge. Nobody at the event had noticed anything was amiss, and Hilary had given the younger woman her card, telling her to call if she needed anything.

"I always wonder how I can pay you back, you know. It's not like I can give you any advice," Kim said.

Hilary laughed. "Well…probably not. But you can pay it forward. Help out somebody new who needs guidance, stuff like that. What we do is hard, and sometimes people think we're just, ah, over-priced coffeemakers, but as you know it's a lot more than that. Otherwise our bosses wouldn't appreciate us. So mentor."

"I will. Thanks again, Hilary.

"My pleasure."

SIX

THE REST OF THE WEEK WENT BY IN THE usual blur. Gavin had cut back, but that didn't mean Hilary's workload had gone down. He focused even more intensely while he was in the office, trying to find efficiencies and get more done in a shorter amount of time. That meant everyone was scrambling to catch up, which wasn't easy. The man was a financial freak. There was a reason why he was considered one of the ten most important figures in a town that worshiped Hollywood. There seemed to be no portfolio he couldn't double in a couple of years, and money, as everyone knew, talked.

It also meant Hilary sometimes worked on Saturdays to catch up, which was exactly how this particular Saturday turned out. She didn't mind. She needed some time away from home anyway.

Her aunt was driving her insane with the "woman's need for a man to complete her" talk. Lila went on with that speech every time she wanted to reminisce about her "good ol' days" with Tim. Hilary had no desire to go to jail for murdering her aunt—so thank god for overtime work.

Around lunch time, Mark strolled into the office carrying a white paper bag. "Hello, beautiful."

He looked clean-cut and gorgeous in a green polo shirt and khakis. His dark hair was mussed like he'd just rolled out of bed. And she had a crazy split-second urge to smooth his hair. "How did you get in?" she asked instead.

"Billy let me through. He knows me."

"You mean you bribed him with a box of donuts."

"It was a *gift*." He put the bag on the sleek carbon fiber chair and rested his hip against the edge of her desk. "How come you're working?"

"Because Gavin needs me here."

"What about me?"

Hilary frowned. "What about you?"

"I need you too."

His delivery was completely deadpan. Heat crept up her chest, and her lips parted. She crossed her arms and curled her hands to contain the tingling feeling at her fingertips. He probably said the same thing to every woman. It was nothing special. "How did you know I was here?"

58

"Gavin told me. I texted you, but you didn't answer."

"Oh. I turned it off to get some work done." Hilary closed the scheduling program. "How can I help you?"

"That may well be the least girlfriend-like thing I've ever heard." He leaned over until their faces were only a few inches apart. "Darling, if we want to convince everyone that we're a real couple, not some fake thing I cooked up to fool my mother, you have to do better."

"Me?" She raised an eyebrow to mask how hard her heart was thumping. It was so loud she was almost certain he could hear it too. "You aren't included in all this?"

"Nope. I'm an expert already." Pulling up a chair, he dumped his two bags on a small table next to her desk and leaned back like he hadn't a care in the world.

"Seriously, why did you decide to come by?"

"We have a date, remember?" He grinned expectantly. It softened his eyes and made him look boyishly charming. His reputation as a player was as bad as his father's, and he'd probably used that smile many times before on numerous women he'd dated. But it still had the power to make her go all soft.

Then her mind registered what he'd just said, and she frowned. "We do?"

"Yes." Leaning forward, he gently flicked the tip

of her nose with his index finger. "The charity event. Surely helping out poor children didn't, you know, slip your mind?"

"Was that today?"

"Yeah, later today so you still have time to prep." Mark glanced at her laptop. "Are you almost done?"

"I need about an hour or so more, but that's it."

"Then let's eat first."

"I don't have time to go out again. I want to get it done and go home. To prep." She was proud of the smooth way she delivered that lie. The last place she wanted to go was home.

"No problem." He pulled out two beautifully packaged deli meals of thinly sliced fish on a bed of sparkling lettuce. "Here you go. Salmon, sea bream and halibut, with lemon and pepper dressing."

"Wow. I didn't know La Mer did takeout."

"It doesn't, but I'm the boss." He grinned. "So I get what I want." He handed her a roll. "Sorry it's not still warm."

"It's fine. It's great." She dug in. Was it a coincidence that he'd brought one of her favorite lunch entrées at the restaurant or had he remembered?

He might be a playboy, but based on how successful he'd been, she'd come to realize he was meticulous when he wanted something. Sloppy and careless people might get lucky once, but they didn't get lucky for close to a decade. And that deserved some respect.

Did he also know Ceinlys had already tried to warn Hilary away from him? She debated, then decided it was better he heard the news from her. "Your mother came to see me a few days ago."

His fork stopped in mid-air, a piece of salmon quivering on the end. All the good humor vanished from his face. "Why didn't you tell me sooner?"

She shrugged, unsure of his mood. There was an odd undercurrent of exasperation and annoyance, but mixed in was something that could only be labeled as long-suffering affection. "She was wondering what my expectations were. She's seen the YouTube video and apparently is worried that I might lead you astray."

He choked and started coughing. She slapped his back vigorously a few times. "Are you okay?"

"Did she ask you to stay away from me?" he asked when he could draw in some air.

"It wasn't like that." She took a small sip of her mineral water to give herself some time. "Your mother probably thought I might have some…unrealistic expectations about you. I told her that wasn't the case at all."

Now he looked slightly offended. "It wasn't? I mean, it isn't?"

"Well… I know your reputation."

"Which is what?"

"That you're your father's son."

Mark met Hilary's frank gaze straight on and knew she hadn't meant to be insulting. He *was* his father's son.

Regret and anger coursed through him. He wanted to snap at Hilary for believing what she'd heard, but why shouldn't she? He really was like that, so what right did he have to be angry with her?

"Mark?" she said, her voice uncertain.

Startled, he blinked. He swallowed his unjustified anger and defaulted to his standard mode. "I'm sure that must've annoyed Mom," he said with a lopsided grin. "She hates being reminded of that."

Hilary's face fell. "I'm sorry. I'm sure it's not something you want to talk about."

"It's all right. It's impossible to be all grown-up and not know about your dad's reputation. Most of us knew before we hit puberty." An intentionally vague way of putting it. He'd known exactly what the situation was since he was six. "Our nannies called them 'your father's female friends.'"

"That's terrible."

"We're used to it."

She reached out and took his hand in hers. "Still…I'm sure it hurts."

He stared at their hands. She'd never initiated contact before, and the fact that she did so to comfort him… He raised his head and looked into her soft eyes in wonder. He couldn't remember the last time somebody had cared enough to do that. But then most people never got this close to him.

Suddenly she flinched and pulled back like she'd just noticed what she'd done. Before he could stop her, she dumped her hands on her lap. A pang of loss pierced his heart, and he shook himself mentally. It was about time he put their lunch back on track. He hadn't come by her office to talk about his past. "Anyway, we have to make our first big splash as a couple."

"Right," she said, almost too eagerly.

"A car will come to pick you up in an hour. Make sure you've got all your stuff done. We don't want Gavin coming after me for distracting you from work. You'll have a team of pros to do your hair and makeup or whatever else you need for the evening. Then we'll fly up to San Francisco and have a great time. You'll probably get to meet my cousin Eliza."

Hilary frowned. "Eliza?"

"Elizabeth Pryce-Reed," he clarified. "I'm the only one who calls her Eliza. This whole charity thing's her deal, and I'm there to lend my support." He finished his salad and threw out his cartons and fork. "By the way, Hilary?"

"Yes?"

"I might not be the Long-Term Prince Forever, but I'll make sure you're happy while we're doing this"—he gestured vaguely—"together until the Fourth of July party."

She looked at him like she wanted to say something, but her lips firmed and she gave him a small nod. "Thanks, Mark. I appreciate the effort."

SEVEN

MARK HADN'T BEEN KIDDING ABOUT THE team of pros to make her pretty for the ball.

The limo driver took her to one of the most exclusive salons in the city. Hilary recognized it from having booked several appointments for Gavin's wife there, but had never used it herself. It was one of those places that didn't list prices on its menu of services; if you had to ask, you couldn't afford it.

A sharply dressed receptionist welcomed her with a smile. Her favorite organic herbal tea appeared like magic, and a stylist dressed all in black who looked skinnier than a flagpole introduced himself and started working on her.

For the next few hours, various professionals fussed over her from hair to makeup to nails. She felt like a slab of meat being prepped for dinner. *My, my, Hilary, aren't you the romantic?*

But she knew that even the pros could do only so much. It wasn't like they could wave their wands and turn her into a size two blonde supermodel. Hilary had tried to diet a few times, but nothing had worked. At this point in her life, she was too stubborn and old to bother. She could never be skinny, but with the right clothes, she could highlight her assets and manage to look fabulous. A small, vain part of her wished she were skinnier…like Gavin's wife, who looked like a model—but minus the supermodel attitude. That way she'd fit in better with the kind of crowd who'd be at Mark's cousin's event.

The fashion coordinator brought out a shimmery off-shoulder white Dior dress in her size. Hilary couldn't help but smile as she put on the dress. She was certain whoever had bought it had had a hard time. Hilary was too curvy for L.A.

Finally they were done. "Come see how you look!" The stylist led her to a room with full-length mirrors on three sides. "What do you think?"

Hilary stared at her reflection, unable to breathe.

She looked like Cinderella before the royal ball. Wisps of curls escaped her artful updo and framed her face, and long diamond earrings shimmered and danced every time she moved her head. The silken material of the dress hugged her curves and made her skin look luminescent. A young assistant brushed some sparkly silvery powder on her shoulders and arms before wrapping a pretty diamond necklace around her neck.

Dramatic makeup accentuated her high cheekbones and eyes. The most romantic shade of glossy pink coated her lips.

"What do you think?" the stylist asked.

"I…wouldn't recognize myself," she whispered in awe. "Thank you. You've turned me into something I could never be on my own."

He chuckled. "Oh please. I wouldn't have been able to work my magic without good raw material. You are gorgeous, Hilary. I just added a few finishing touches, nothing particularly difficult. Enjoy your evening."

The limo driver opened the door for her. If he noticed the transformation, he didn't say. The receptionist handed him a large black bag containing Hilary's old shoes and clothes as she settled into the car. When he climbed behind the wheel, she asked, "Where's Mark?"

"Mr. Pryce is at the airport, Miss Rosenberg."

"Call me Hilary."

"Yes, ma'am."

She winced at how aloof and stiff the guy was. He raised the partition between them as he pulled the car into the traffic, and she sat back. She shouldn't let it get to her. It wasn't like it mattered whether Mark's driver approved of her. This date was her returning a favor. That was all.

That was all.

Everything would go back to the way it had been in a month. Oddly, the thought didn't cheer her up nearly as much as she expected it to.

AT THE HANGAR, MARK ROLLED HIS SHOULDERS, trying to relieve the tension gathering there. "Is there something wrong with the tuxedo, sir?" the cabin attendant asked. She gave him a concerned smile and ran her hand along his back.

He shrugged away her touch. "It's fine." The tux was from Italy and impeccably tailored. He shooed her away and turned his attention back to the call from his brother. "So you're going too?"

"Basically," Iain said.

"I can't believe Mom's dragging you to the concert. She doesn't even like classical music."

"I know. It's because of you. She was fine with not going until she heard you were taking Hilary. Then all of a sudden I got stuck with escorting her to San Francisco."

Their father already had a date for the concert, of course—Salazar Pryce didn't attend social functions solo. What had happened to all Ceinlys's comfort men? Or was she being extra discreet to avoid any ugliness? She was careful about not giving her husband any reason to divorce her. The Pryce prenup had effectively leashed her, changing her in the process, and Mark felt the familiar sorrow and resentment tighten his throat. His dad should've suffered just as much if not more. "How did she get tickets?"

"Elizabeth hooked her up."

"Damn. Things might get awkward. Hilary told me Mom tried to warn her away already."

"Sucks to be you," Iain said, not entirely unsympathetic. "Now that I've warned you, my brotherly duty is done. I have to get my jet ready. See you in a few hours."

Mark hung up and brooded. Maybe it wouldn't matter that much. Eliza was shrewd enough to keep Ceinlys, Salazar and Mark away from each other. But why was his mother so against Hilary? Was it because she reminded Ceinlys of her past? She'd been a great beauty but without a penny to her name—his paternal grandmother had frequently pointed out that *significant* flaw when he was growing up.

"A common working girl was what your mother was," Shirley Pryce had often said, her voice surprisingly strong for a woman her age. "If it hadn't been for her pretty face, she would've never been able to trap your father. He could've married a well-bred heiress from a great family, not somebody like her."

"Are you angry with me, Grandma?" he'd asked when he was seven.

Her forehead creased as she raised her eyebrows. "Angry with you? For what, my dear?"

"Because of my mom. If Dad married somebody better, I might have turned out better too."

"Don't be silly, my little angel. You're the greatest grandson I could ever ask for." She'd smiled and worried one of his cheeks in that special way she had that made him laugh. But then her eyes had focused on something only she could see. "We can always right our course. We'll make sure you marry the right sort of woman."

His grandmother might be dead and gone, but her vow seemed to have survived. He was certain his mother didn't know about the conversation, but she was nevertheless trying to herd him in exactly the same direction. She despised working women, as if she'd forgotten where she'd come from.

He rocked on his feet, waiting for Hilary's limo to show. Was he putting her in a bad position? His mother didn't take kindly to people who got in her way, and she could be spiteful when she was angry. He didn't want her to take it out on Hilary.

He would be lying if he said he wasn't intrigued by her. She was sexy, not to mention smart. She'd fascinated him for months, and he'd never waited this long to date a woman before. Would that fact make any difference? Or would he grow bored with her, too…just like he had with all his exes?

When the car finally pulled in, he took a deep breath. The driver opened the door, Hilary stepped out and…

Mark couldn't remember what had gotten him so anxious.

Hilary was a vision in shimmering white. The dress clung in all the right places, accentuating the beautiful curves of her womanly body. When she met his eyes and gave him a shy little smile, it was as though all the air had suddenly been sucked out of the hangar. His heart quickened, and all he could see was her.

And in that moment, he finally understood what men meant when they said they'd slay a dragon for a woman. The knowledge twisted something inside him. His feelings for her wouldn't last. He couldn't imagine them changing, but his past said they would because…he was who he was.

He wished he weren't Mark Pryce, a man unable to love a woman the way she deserved to be loved. He didn't know how even if he wanted to. He'd never had a role model to emulate.

It didn't matter what he felt right now. This "relationship" would ultimately end in a month. So why not try to keep her as a friend at least? He could get through this, with his mother placated and Hilary kept at enough of a distance that she wouldn't think of him with bitterness when it was all over.

Keep it light. Keep it simple. Don't hurt anybody.

"Hi," she said, her voice low and husky.

"Hey. You look gorgeous."

A delicate flush colored her skin. "Thanks."

"Shall we?" He extended an arm.

"Of course." Instead of placing her hand in his elbow, she linked her fingers with his. He drew in a sharp breath, then after a moment, squeezed her hand. There was something so gentle and sweet about the way their fingers were entwined...he felt weightless, like all the burdens he carried had vanished.

EIGHT

THE CONCERT WAS THE GRANDEST THING Hilary had ever attended. She'd heard of private charity concerts, but had never attended one. From years of working for Gavin, she recognized almost everyone there. Her boss was there with his wife, and next to them sat his brother Ethan and his wife Kerri. Both the couples were as close as they could be without sitting on each other's laps. Kerri had her head on Ethan's broad shoulder and a hand on his chest as she watched the orchestra. There was something so intimate and sweet about their love. Longing created a little pang in Hilary's heart, and she swallowed. She should remember to be grateful for all that she'd accomplished on her own—despite where she'd come from—and just enjoy the moment.

"Did you like it?" Mark asked after the performance was over.

"I loved it. Oh wow." She gave him a big grin. After years of setting Gavin's social calendar for him, she was finally experiencing a high society date herself. "Thank you. It was beautiful."

He grinned back at her. "My pleasure." He kissed the back of her hand. She shivered at how soft his mouth felt there, and how the little touch made her insides throb. She smiled even more brightly.

The crowd moved to a giant hall set up for a special reception. Bright crystals dripped from numerous chandeliers. The shiny marble floor showed a blurry reflection of the angels and clouds painted on the domed ceiling, and tuxedoed servers wove through the guests to offer them refreshments. Everyone had donated at least twenty thousand dollars to the cause to build schools in some poor country in Africa. Eliza Pryce-Reed was a shrewd fundraiser, and apparently educating and feeding children was her thing.

Standing by Mark's side, Hilary sipped a glass of champagne and watched the who's-who of high society mingle. They chatted like they were all best friends, and people greeted each other so sweetly. Everyone was dressed to be seen and noted. Hilary was certain of it. The perfume in the air alone had to cost more than twenty thousand dollars.

A group of people came by to sweep Mark away to get his thought on some venture they were trying to get off the ground. "I shouldn't leave my date," he said.

A middle-aged man took a long look at Hilary. "She can come with you I suppose."

"No, it's all right," she said. Most men weren't comfortable talking business freely in the presence of a woman they didn't know well. "Go ahead."

Mark turned to Hilary. "You sure?"

She nodded. "I'll just go out and get some fresh air while you do your thing."

"I'll be back as soon as I can." He dropped a quick kiss on the top of her head.

After he was gone, she stood by the veranda railing. The night glittered with the lights of the city. It was interesting to be at the same social event as her boss, but as a guest rather than some type of support staff. And it was intriguing to observe the way all these wealthy and famous people treated Mark. She'd thought he was popular and good at operating restaurants. But apparently his talents extended beyond that since several people had wanted his opinion on various investments they were considering.

She took a deep breath of the cool evening air, trying to relax. Yeah, Mark was gorgeous, smart and funny. That only made him more impossible for her. Even if he hadn't been a playboy—and the son of a playboy—he was totally out of her league.

She was a Rosenberg girl. When she was growing up, adults had looked at her with pity and contempt, certain she'd end up just like her mother. Kids had been worse. They'd spat on her and kicked her and called her horrible names. All of them had known she wasn't worth anything, and it was all she could manage to claw herself out of the fate everyone had been sure would be hers. But that wasn't enough to date somebody like Mark.

"Whew." A man came onto the veranda and sighed. "Do you mind if I hide out here for a bit?"

"Not at all," she said, bemused and glad for a distraction. He looked just like Mark except for the dark eyes. And his exceptionally clean and classic profile confirmed her suspicion. "Are you one of the Pryce brothers?"

"Yeah. Iain." He gave her a long stare. "You're Hilary Rosenberg, right?"

"Yes," she said, a little surprised.

"I've heard a lot about you."

"Hopefully it was mostly complimentary." Then she remembered the YouTube video and winced inwardly. Maybe not.

He gave her a lopsided grin that looked remarkably like Mark's. But Iain didn't make her breath catch or insides warm. "Don't worry. So, did he beg you to save him from having to date and possibly marry the dreaded heiress?" His eyes sparkled. "I hope you made him get on his knees. You deserve at least that much."

Self-conscious, she laughed. "Stop teasing."

"Do I look like the teasing type to you?" He leaned against the railing and they looked out over the city lights. "I'm always serious about women."

"Mmm. The way Mark is, I'm sure."

He turned his head and studied her. "You're pretty direct."

"Is there any point in not being direct?"

"I suppose not." He gave her another easy smile. "I can see why my brother's into you. You're more interesting than Katarina. So why are you hiding out here? Do you need some solitude away from my no-good brother?"

"No, it's because some finance guys stole me away from her," Mark said from behind them. His hands settled around her waist, and it was all she could do to not melt into his warmth. "If you stay here much longer, Mom's going to track you down. You know how she is."

Iain sighed. "Yeah, you're right. I should've followed Dane's example and just run off."

"Ah, but the heir is poised to return," Mark said in a pompous announcer's voice, "so you'll be safe again soon enough."

Hilary tilted her head and looked up at Mark. "When?"

"In a few weeks for the Fourth of July party."

And based on what Kim had said, he wouldn't be going back to wherever he lived. That was much faster than Hilary had expected.

"Come on. Let's go back in and mingle." Mark lowered his head and whispered into her ear, "I want us to be seen. I want everyone to know you're mine."

Mine.

Her stomach fluttered at such a possessive word. Warmth started at the small of her back where his hand still rested and spread to the rest of her. She wanted to lean just a little bit closer to him, angle her body just so, but she swallowed hard and resisted the urge. This was a make-believe relationship. After it was over, he'd return to what he did best—going from one Quarterly Girl to another. Everyone here probably knew she was one…except she was only going to last a month.

Did they pity her?

Despite her apprehensions, everyone Mark introduced her to was gracious. Most knew who she was—Gavin's trusted assistant. That probably helped, since most people knew how much her boss liked her, and not many people wanted to offend Gavin.

Toward the end of the event, Hilary slipped away to the ladies' room. Maybe she shouldn't have drunk so much, but it was difficult to resist the best champagne and cocktails money could buy, and waiters had ensured she was never empty-handed.

As she was finishing up in a stall, she heard a few women walk in. One of them sniffed loudly, while two others moved around, their shoes clacking against the tiled floor.

"Did you see that redheaded cow he brought here?" Woman Number One said, sniffing again.

"I know. What an ass. And I don't mean hers. I can't believe he downgraded. What does he see in her?"

"He must like them shameless. Did you see how she was strutting around? Where did she even find a Dior that huge? I'm surprised her heels don't break under all that weight."

"He could take her down to Texas. Every other step and she'd strike oil."

There was tittering laughter. Hilary put her hands on her suddenly hot cheeks.

"Crap. I can't find my lipstick," a third woman said.

Some rustling and clattering, and Woman Number Two said, "Try mine. It's almost the same shade."

"Thanks." A short pause. "It galls me how people can't see what she really is. For god's sake, she's a secretary."

"Yup. Bet she got her job because she's good at…"

Hilary strained to hear what the other woman was saying, but obviously she wasn't going to say it out loud. Or maybe Hilary just couldn't hear over the roar of her blood in her ears.

A moment later all the women burst out laughing. "Oh my god! Who would want that from somebody who looks like her?"

"Some men like them chubby. Besides, she has that trashy look going on."

"I wouldn't be surprised if her family's been on one of those daytime talk shows." Woman Number Two put on a twangy accent. "'How could you fuck mah sister while you were wit *me*? Ah even had your *baybee!*'"

The ensuing giggles sounded garbled and distant as spots appeared in Hilary's vision. How could they know? Was it that obvious? It was shameful to admit, but the fact was both her mother and aunt would've been more than happy to be on one of those programs. She could just imagine them, twin sisters fighting over who deserved Tim more... except he'd been generally unavailable for that kind of confrontation. There had been too many women to screw to bother with TV.

"...let her enjoy her Cinderella moment," Woman Number Three was saying. "Soon the clock's going to strike midnight. You know Mark. She'll be lucky to last one month, much less three."

"No shit. Taylor, you'll get him back."

"Oh, I plan to," Woman Number One said.

The voices dwindled as the three women exited.

Her knees weak, Hilary opened the door of the stall and peered out. Her reflection stared back from the big mirror, and suddenly her entire ensemble— the dress, the earrings, her make-up, everything— looked ludicrous, like expensive window dressing on a dime-store mannequin.

The women were wrong. She wasn't even Cinderella. In the fairy tale, everyone thought she was a princess…because deep down, Cinderella was a princess kind of girl. Hilary wasn't like that. It didn't matter what she wore or whose arm she was gracing. She could never hide who she was. What she was.

She was a messed up girl from a messed up family. She didn't belong here.

MARK COULD TELL SOMETHING WAS WRONG THE instant Hilary returned from the bathroom. She was so pale, not even the makeup could hide it. "Hey, you all right?" He took her hand, and the iciness of her skin shocked him. Her eyes were glazed, but it couldn't have been from drinking. She'd been fine when she left. "Hilary, baby, talk to me. Are you all right?"

"I don't feel so good." She rubbed a finger against her temple. "I want to go home."

"Yeah, sure. Of course." He made some excuse to Eliza—she promised to see him again at the family party—and escorted Hilary out. The driver waited outside with their limo.

Hilary shivered in the car, and Mark put his jacket around her. What the hell had happened to make her like this? She'd seemed to be having a good time, and everyone they'd met had been gracious and sweet…except his ex, Taylor, who'd somehow managed to wrangle an invitation. Eliza had apologized profusely for the awkwardness, but whatever. It wasn't like Taylor didn't know the score, and she'd behaved herself even if her eyes had flashed daggers at Hilary. Stupid girl. If she'd been smarter, she would've known their breakup had nothing to do with Hilary.

Still…

"Hey, did something happen back there? Somebody say something to you?" he asked. If it was Taylor, he'd throttle her.

Hilary started. "No. Nothing like that. I just have a headache."

He put an arm around her, and she flinched. "Sorry," she said, then gave him a wan smile. "I sort of ruined it, didn't I?"

He wanted to know what made her pull away like that, but she was trying so hard to put on a brave face that he didn't have the heart to push her on it. It was obvious she was barely hanging on, and he could sense control was important to her. So he forced a lighter tone. "Ruin what?"

"You know…the function. Whatever. You need to mingle and be seen."

"Nah. Eliza doesn't care so long as she gets my money. I'm just a mobile ATM as far as she's concerned."

Hilary's eyes widened. "Seriously?"

"No. I'm kidding. She likes me, but yeah, she also hits me up for money a lot. It's for a good cause, so I don't mind too much."

Hilary's place was a rather humble house located in a lower middle-class neighborhood. Strange. Mark knew she could afford something nicer than this. The commute alone would be pretty awful, given how far it was from Gavin's downtown office.

They pulled up, and a moment later the door opened, the chauffeur standing by like a sentinel. She put a hand on Mark's arm. "You don't have to get out. I can walk myself."

"But…" How could he argue with those pleading eyes? She looked like she'd shatter if anybody even breathed wrong around her. Against his better judgment, he nodded. "Okay, but I'm swinging by tomorrow to check up on you."

"I'm fine."

"We'll see."

She started to shrug his jacket off, but he stopped her. "Take it. That's the least you can do after destroying my hopes and dreams for the evening."

She gave a small laugh, but stepped out with his jacket. It settled around her like a lover's embrace, and he wished he were wrapped around her instead. Then he could press his lips to hers and warm her with his heat.

It was a desire he'd had more than a few times in his life, with more than a few women. But for some reason it went deeper this time, with an emotional undertone that felt foreign. And he found that bothered him.

NINE

WATCHING THE LIMO DISAPPEAR, HILARY pulled the jacket closer. It smelled so good...like Mark. She could almost pretend it was his arms around her.

What a crazy thought. The two of them weren't going to end up together. No matter how she viewed the situation, those women in the bathroom had been right. She didn't belong with him. At least Cinderella was a well-born girl down on her luck. There was nothing well-born about Hilary or her family.

She started toward the house, then stopped when a man jumped out of a car. Her eyes widened when she recognized Walt and his Lexus.

"Hilary!" he said, approaching her rapidly. His shirt and slacks were rumpled. His prematurely graying hair stuck up in clumps, which was unusual. He always looked so professional and doctor-like.

"What are you doing here?" she asked, tightening her hold around the jacket.

"I've been trying all night to get in touch with you."

Her phone had been turned off for the concert, and she hadn't turned it back on yet. "What's there to talk about?"

"Look, I don't know what happened, but I don't have a fiancée."

"What?"

"I'm saying... Shit." He raked his hair, messing it up further. "I saw the YouTube video. A colleague told me about it, and I was like what the hell?"

"Walt, it happened over a week ago, and you just found out?"

"I was out of the country for a conference. I told you that."

"Yes, you did. You were always really great about telling me when you weren't going to be around." Something bitter spread in her chest. "So thoughtful."

"You don't seriously believe her, do you? I swear to you, I've never seen that woman before."

"Well *I* certainly don't know her. So...what? You want me to believe that some woman neither one of us has ever seen before suddenly decided to see if she could break us up? Just for shits and grins? Is that really what you're asking me to buy?" Her pent-up fury, fear and humiliation shattered her control. If he hadn't been a two-timing bastard, she wouldn't have been subjected to the scene at her company lobby. Nor would she have gone out with Mark…and heard all those horrible things about herself. She fisted her hands and glared at him. "Because if you are, I've got a better scenario. You're here because your fiancée dumped you for cheating on her, and now you want to see what you can salvage out of the mess!"

"Hilary—"

"Just stop. There's nothing you can do to change any of it. It's over, Walt."

"But—"

"I thought you were different. I thought you were one of the few good guys."

"I *am* a good guy!"

"No, you're not. You're a horrible jerk. Did I look so easy to you? Was there something on my forehead that said, 'This woman's okay to fool around with on the side, while my fiancée sits at home thinking I'm out there saving some baby's life?'"

Walt pulled back like he'd been struck. Then he looked at her up and down, as if he'd just noticed her clothes. "I see. So this woman has provided you with convenient, guilt-free permission to move on. Who did you latch onto? Your boss?"

"Are you crazy? He's married!"

"Why would that matter to you?"

"It means everything to me! I'm not like some people."

"Girls like you... Why wouldn't you want to marry well? You know the kind of life they can give you. You see it up close every day. I remember you talking about the jet your boss gave his wife. I..." His mouth tightened. "I'll never be able to give you that."

"This isn't about money or private jets, Walt. It's about you cheating." *Me picking the wrong guy again.*

"I told you I don't know the woman. This is all about *you*"—he pointed at Hilary—"willing to dump *me* so you can move on to something better. And if your boss isn't available, what did you do? Snatch one of his rich clients and friends?"

Hilary stiffened. "You are *not* making this about me."

"I have a better idea. Let's not make it about either of us anymore. I want the bracelet back."

"Oh, so the real reason for this visit comes out."

"It belonged to my mother. It's for a woman who's true and deserving, not somebody like you."

Bitterness and anger flooded her. He was the one in the wrong, but somehow it was she who was unworthy of anything better. "Sue me."

She turned to go. He caught her wrist. "Don't do this," he ground out.

She gave him a cold stare. "Let go or I'll call cops for harassment and sic an army of lawyers on you." When his grip tightened, she lost her temper. "You don't think I'll do it? Like you said, I found myself a rich boyfriend. And he will be more than happy to drag you all over the court system for me."

Walt released her. "Bitch."

She rubbed her wrist. "Well, that's original." She'd heard worse. She'd called herself worse.

He stalked off, and she took a deep shuddering breath. *I guess that was slightly better than the situation in college.* Walt had at least tried to deny everything, and acted like he was somewhat horrified. Freddie hadn't had that much decency. No, he'd actually been pleased to have been caught in her bed with her cousin, both of them buck naked.

Hilary shook her head. She should erase Freddie from her memory. He wasn't worth it. Never had been. The only thing he'd wanted was to fuck both Rosenberg girls at the same time. He'd known the whole sordid story—how she and Bebe were cousins, but also half-sisters who looked enough alike to practically be twins. That plus the Rosenberg women's reputation for being loose…

She slipped into the house and climbed upstairs to her bedroom. Aunt Lila used the master suite, and she had the second largest room in the house. It used to belong to Bebe, but since she was gone, Hilary hadn't seen any reason to stay in the smallest one.

Opening the door to her room, she flicked on the light switch and let out a small yelp at an unfamiliar lump on her bed. As it shifted, the blanket lowered, and Bebe's sleepy face looked at her. "Hey, cuz."

"Bebe? Good god, what are you doing here?"

She shrugged. "Sleeping, what else?"

"Uh, this is my room now."

"Sorry. Didn't know."

"Uh huh. All the office clothes didn't give it away? The new bed?"

"Don't be such a bitch, Hilary. It's not like you."

"Come on, out," Hilary said, jerking a thumb over her shoulder. "You can sleep in my old room now that you know."

"But it's so small," Bebe whined.

"Maybe you shouldn't have run off. Then you could've kept this one."

"I didn't 'run off.' I was on an adventure. Of self-discovery." Bebe got up. She was naked except for a thong so tiny it shouldn't count. She had long red hair like Hilary, but instead of letting it cover herself, she tossed it over her shoulders. "I look good, don't I? These are new tats." She traced swirly lines etched onto her breasts. "Wanna closer look?"

Repulsed, Hilary almost took a step back. "No! Get out."

"Don't be such a prude." Bebe gave her a speculative look. "Are you still pissed off about Freddie?"

"No." Hilary would never admit how much that

betrayal had hurt her. But her cousin knew her too well. They had grown up together.

"God, Hilary, it was decades ago. Honestly, aren't you sorry you missed out on a chance for a hot threesome? It would've been pretty sweet."

Hilary couldn't believe Bebe's gall. Her stomach knotted until she thought she might throw up—the same thing she'd felt when she'd discovered Bebe and Freddie in her bed. The old pain and humiliation formed a tight fist around her throat. "Aren't you even *a little* ashamed of yourself?" she choked out. "Don't you feel any guilt that you stole my boyfriend?"

"Hey, he knew what he wanted, and so did I. You're the one who bailed. I didn't steal anything. For fuck's sake, I didn't keep him afterward. I only wanted him for a good time, and if you weren't going to join, there was no point." Bebe's gaze swept over Hilary. "Speaking of which… Isn't that a man's jacket? How about this time then? You were mad I didn't tell you beforehand. So I'm telling you now—"

"Bebe, shut up." Mark was so much more special than Freddie. Hilary didn't know what she'd do if that nightmarish scene played out with Mark in it. "If you go near him, I'll kill you."

"Don't be such a greedy bitch," Bebe snapped. "It doesn't matter where you work, how much money you make or how up-scale you dress. You aren't that special, Hilary. We all share the same blood and the same daddy. We are all the fucking same!" She marched past Hilary and left. A door opened and slammed.

Her legs like wet noodles, Hilary leaned against the wall and slowly slid down to the floor. Tears prickled her eyes, and she covered her mouth to contain a sob. Bebe was wrong. Hilary was *not* like the women in her family. She knew the destructive power of living high on drama.

And she understood the madness of trusting men, relying on them, equating sex with anything more. She'd done everything in her power to ensure she wouldn't repeat the mistakes her mom and aunt had made. The men she'd dated inspired affection, but not passion. Her clothes were conservative— and fashionable enough, according to Jo—to ensure she'd project the proper image of a serious-minded career woman. She'd chosen the best job she could based on her skills, and she'd worked tirelessly to make sure she was indispensable.

Still…

The women in the bathroom had known, hadn't they? They could tell Hilary wasn't like them, that she was messed up like her mom and aunt and Bebe. Others might be too polite to say anything to her face, but how many had thought it? Those three couldn't be the only ones.

Hilary rested her forehead on her bent knees, making herself as small as possible. She was going to be okay. She wasn't going to be like the women in her family. She would work even harder to hide what she was, so people would never find out.

So Mark would never find out.

TEN

THE NEXT MORNING, MARK WAS SCOWLING as he munched his breakfast cereal at the kitchen counter of his downtown penthouse. The gorgeous view of the California morning, normally a source of pleasure, did nothing for his mood. It bugged him Hilary hadn't wanted him to walk her to her door the night before, and that she'd looked so small and sad standing there on the street as he'd driven away.

Damn it. Instead of worrying about her control and dignity, he should've pushed until she told him what was wrong.

He pulled out his phone and called Eliza. He had a feeling Hilary would never tell him now that his chance was gone, but his cousin might have heard something. She knew everything that happened at her events.

"Oh my gosh, do you know what time it is?" she moaned.

"Seven thirty. Why?"

"I didn't get to bed until almost four."

"Hope he was worth it."

"There was no 'he,' you perv."

"In that case, my condolences."

"Condolences? *Condolences?* That's all you have to say?"

"Eliza, you know you're my favorite cousin. And as much as I'd love to let you sleep the morning away, I need to talk to you about something. Did you notice anything odd last night?"

"What do you mean?"

He told her about Hilary's unexplainable mood the night before. "See? Kind of strange, don't you think?"

"It is. She seemed to be having a great time. Even Taylor was behaving. I was kind of worried she might make a scene…apparently she was really upset when you dumped her."

"I didn't *dump* her," he said. "We parted amicably." That was the story he was sticking to, more for Taylor's sake than his.

"Not what I heard. I was told a few insults were involved."

"Well, 'insults.' She didn't realize her time would be so short and vocalized her shock." He'd broken up with her after two months rather than the usual three. But he hadn't been able to bring himself to stay with her for even one more hour.

Eliza snorted. "Is that what we call four-letter words these days?"

"Her favorite words had seven and, um…ten letters. But hey, I gave her diamond earrings as a 'sorry to break up so early' gift."

"I'm sure that made it all better."

"Well, she kept them. She even said hello to me last night. So she can't be that mad."

"Honestly, I don't know how you get away with your antics, Mark. I'll see what I can find out. If anybody was less than polite to Hilary, I'll know and make sure they're blacklisted."

"Really?" He hadn't expected his warm and laid-back cousin to volunteer such a harsh response.

"I like Hilary. She's…nice. And normal and down to earth. I never thought to see you date somebody like her."

"Hey! I date nice girls all the time."

"Surface nice. I was going to start calling you Ken if you brought home another of your Barbie girlfriends."

"They were never that bad."

"Were too. Skinny blondes with enormous fake ta-tas have always been your type…but I'm glad you're growing out of that. Anyway, is Hilary there with you? She's awfully quiet, and I feel terrible, talking about her like she isn't there."

"Don't worry. She's not here."

There was a pause. "Well, that's a surprise. She dump you already?"

"No," he ground out. Why did Eliza think such a thing? He hated how people just assumed Hilary would dump him at any moment. Especially when they were smart people. "If you must know, I dropped her off at her place last night."

A longer moment of silence. "All right, Martian impostor. What have you done with my cousin?"

"Oh come on."

"*You* come on. There's no way you just let her go like that. You slept with her, right? Then went home? It's not like you to play friends without benefits."

"I didn't and haven't," he said, trying for a touch of asperity. The light, fun tone he employed so successfully with women didn't work on Hilary. On the other hand, he hated "serious." Serious meant the possibility of commitment. Maybe when he found a woman who didn't get boring after twelve weeks he might try serious. But until then he was keeping things light and simple. He didn't want to hurt anybody, especially Hilary. "I'm not that kind of boy."

The laughter on the other end of the line went on so long he put the phone down on the counter and turned on the speaker function. "Are you losing your touch?" Eliza asked, after she caught her breath.

He looked up at the ceiling. "Didn't you say you wanted to go back to sleep?"

"Uh-huh." She yawned. "But this is just too juicy. You, heading home alone after a date." She started laughing again.

"Go back to bed. There's nothing juicy. It's sleep deprivation making you hallucinate juicy."

She chuckled. "All right. Just don't go join a monastery or anything, okay?" She hung up amid more gales of laughter.

He scowled at his phone. His relationships were never with Barbie-women. He'd always chosen his girlfriends because they were interesting.

It wasn't his fault they became boring so quickly.

Then something else occurred to him. Hilary was pretending to go out with him so he could avoid getting set up with that heiress. But if they stopped seeing each other after the Fourth of July, people would assume she couldn't hang onto him for more than four weeks.

Shit. That didn't sit well. She deserved more than that. Maybe he'd stage a fake breakup scene where she could dump him.

After a quick shower, he put on a blue shirt and khaki shorts. The night before had ended on a dis-appointing note, but it had given him some useful information: where Hilary lived.

Almost an hour later, he pulled into her driveway. It was already nine thirty, so she should be up by now. Or so he'd hoped since she hadn't picked up her phone. Maybe she'd just gotten up. He smiled at the idea. Women looked so soft and sweet when they'd just woken up, their eyes languid and their cheeks flushed.

A moment after he rang, the door opened, revealing a woman who looked remarkably like Hilary in build, height and coloring. But that was where their similarities ended. She had a hard-edged mien that said she'd seen and done things outside the experience of most women. The glint in her eyes hinted she might have enjoyed some of them.

She was barely decent. Her big breasts pushed against a thin white tank-top, and he could see the faint outline of her nipples. The ripped denim shorts were so short, he'd be able to see the under-curves of her butt cheeks if she turned around. She stretched one arm along the door frame and smiled at him. "Well, hello."

"Hi. Is Hilary here?" he asked, keeping his gaze above her neck.

"No, she's out." She gave him a vampish smile. "But I'm here. Who are you?"

"Mark. Is she out for—"

"Mark," she repeated, like she was testing the name. She tapped her lower lip with a finger, then wiped the lipstick on her shorts. "Are you the one who gave her that nice jacket last night?"

"Yeah. About—"

She snapped her fingers. "I knew it! I'm Bebe." She put her hand out. "Nice to meet you."

Despite his impatience, good manners kicked in and he shook her hand. "Pleasure. Are you her sister? She never said."

She laughed like he'd said something too precious. "Sister? Oh my god." Her hand flew to her stomach, and she doubled over, chortling.

O-kay. This was weird. "If Hilary's not here…" He turned around and started to leave.

"Wait!"

He glanced back at the still-laughing woman. "Yes?"

"Nothing. I see I did her a big favor. I had no idea she'd trade up to something this nice." She wiped her tears. "If you wanna see her, try her friend's place. Josephine Martinez. Or the owm office. It's not like Hilary has a life or a place to be other than those two."

Mark doubted Hilary was at the office. So Josephine's place it was. Thankfully he knew where she lived since she sometimes worked with his family.

"DRINK THIS." JO PUT A BIG GLASS OF ICED COFFEE in front of Hilary. "You look like shit."

Count on her friend to be honest. On the other hand, Hilary had to look awful after tossing and turning all night long. And she'd spent only a few minutes putting on some powder and lipstick that morning.

"What happened?" Jo asked.

"I should've never agreed to go to the charity thing with Mark. I should've just joined a convent." Hilary drank the coffee deeply. As the caffeine kicked in, she felt almost normal. "You think it's too late?"

"For what?"

"To be a nun."

Jo pretended to give it some thought. "Gavin will do everything in his power to stop you. He probably has the Pope on speed-dial, given how he seems to know everyone." She took the seat next to Hilary. "And you like food too much. Don't they only eat bread and water in convents?"

"The charity event was terrible." Hilary sighed. "I made a fool of myself, and I'm sure a lot of people there think I'm some terrible skank or something."

"*You?* Ha. I had to spend days to convince you to wear real shoes. If it weren't for me, you'd have the most drab sense of style ever. The invisible woman."

"I wish." Hilary moaned and buried her face in the crook of her arm. The three in the bathroom had seen through everything. "Walt confronted me last night."

Jo gasped. "That rat bastard? What did he have to say?"

"He wanted the bracelet back." Hilary lifted her head. "Apparently it's an heirloom."

"What a dumbass. He shouldn't have given it to you then."

"I know, right?"

"Did you tell him to shove it?"

"More or less. He said he has no idea who the woman in the YouTube video is."

Jo started laughing. "Oh my god, that's rich. Was he serious? He wasn't on crack or something?"

"Definitely serious. But that's not all of it."

"There's more?"

"Bebe's in town."

The snarky humor vanished from Jo's eyes, and her mouth set in a tight line. "Uh oh. Since when?"

"Sometime yesterday, I guess. She was in my room when I got back."

"What was she doing there?"

"Sleeping…allegedly."

"She's such a piece of work. You want something a little more therapeutic than coffee? One of my clients came back from Russia and brought me a bottle of vodka. It's good stuff."

"No, it's fine. I'm just trying to wrap my head around all this." Or more like not let her head explode all over it. "Why would she come back after all this time?"

"Probably to cause trouble. She's still wild, isn't she?"

Hilary nodded. "Same old Bebe. She was virtually naked in my bed."

"Ewww."

"And really in my face about everything. You know… Freddie."

"What a bitch."

Hilary pressed her fingers to her eyes, which were dry and irritated. Thank god she'd put on glasses instead of contacts. "I can't even…" She sighed. "She was rubbing it in. I'm sure she didn't crawl into my bed without a reason."

"Of course not. God, I hate her."

Jo knew the humiliating end to Hilary's sordid relationship with Freddie. He'd seemed so perfect… so true and genuine…until she'd gone to her dorm room and found him screwing Bebe in Hilary's own bed. She'd expected him to apologize, maybe even grovel and try to explain what the hell he thought he was doing. But he hadn't been sorry. He'd been offended Hilary hadn't wanted to join them. "Come on! You're a Rosenberg," he had said. "I know all about you and your family."

The scene had reminded Hilary of her mother and aunt's relationship with Tim. How dysfunctional and destructive that had been for both women. Her mother had died precisely because she hadn't learned how to live on her own and take care of herself. After Tim had gotten himself killed in a car accident, she'd more or less poisoned herself with drugs.

Hilary wasn't going to end up like that.

A gentle touch of Jo's hand on Hilary's shoulder pulled her out of her dark memories. "Hey," Jo said. "Do you want to crash at my place until Bebe takes off again?"

That was a definite possibility. "Are you sure? She might not leave for a while."

"I'm sure. Hilary, you really need to stay away from that toxic family of yours. They aren't good for you, and being around them only brings you down. Trust me on this."

Hilary forced a small smile, touched at her friend's concern. But leaving her aunt was easier said than done. As the only blood relative who was around with any consistency, she felt responsible for Lila. "Thanks. I owe you one."

"No, no, no. You don't owe me anything. What I'm doing is what any good friend's supposed to do. You'd do the same for me."

"Still. Thank you."

"And—" Her intercom buzzed and Jo frowned. "Hold on." She went to answer it, and Hilary used the time to gather herself. She shouldn't let Bebe's reappearance get to her. Her cousin was manipulative and liked to screw with people. But Hilary didn't have to play that game.

Jo came back with a bemused smile. "That was Mark."

"Mark?" Hilary blinked. "What does he want?"

"You. He heard you were here."

"How?"

"No idea. But he's coming up right now." Jo dipped into her purse and pulled out a tube of concealer. "Here. Let me put some of this on you." She dabbed a little on Hilary's dark circles. "My lord," she muttered, "you need to take better care of yourself and not let that bitch cousin of yours get to you like this. She's just jealous, you know. She's in her late thirties, and has nothing. No friend, no job, no prospects. Don't let her ruin your happiness. She's not worth it." Jo pulled back and looked at Hilary's face critically. "Much better. Now you don't look like you spent all night worrying about some worthless ho."

Hilary gave her friend a tremulous smile. As silly and vain as it was, she didn't want to look awful, even if she was just fake-dating Mark. She'd seen the photos of his exes. They were all drop-dead gorgeous.

The doorbell rang, and Jo went over to open it. Hilary's breath caught at how beautiful Mark looked in a casual shirt and shorts. No matter what he wore, there was a certain male elegance and power that came through.

"Hey, Josephine, thanks for letting me in to steal her," he said with an easy grin and gave Hilary a friendly nod. Josephine didn't allow any of her clients to call her Jo. She said that would make her sound too…common.

"You're welcome. And hey, nice shirt. You need to hire me more often."

"Don't worry, I will. And I'll get my sister to do the same."

She gestured toward the kitchen. "She's all yours. Treat her well or you'll hear from me."

"Yes, ma'am," he said teasingly. He came into the kitchen and gave Hilary's hand a gentle squeeze.

As he pulled away, she sank her teeth into her lower lip. Mark wasn't like Freddie or Walt. He was a lot more attractive than either of them—devastating, really—and didn't just inspire affection, but a genuine longing for more…except she knew she couldn't have it. She was a Rosenberg girl, and Bebe's return had reminded her of her origins. Mark was…well, he was the sun. A messed up girl from a messed up family shouldn't even dream of being near him. He would incinerate her if she wasn't careful.

Ignoring a foolish whisper that told her to lean on him, she kept her spine straight. She knew the score—Mark was a short-term guy, and she would be wise to remember that. Leaning on men for anything more invited nothing but misery.

ELEVEN

MARK COULDN'T PUZZLE OUT WHAT MADE Hilary so stiff. Not that he expected her to turn into a puddle of goo whenever she saw him. But he was a pretty charming guy, and a lot of women did just that. He didn't understand why Hilary was an exception; he could tell she didn't find him repulsive or anything.

As a matter of fact, he was certain she found him attractive. She'd said he was his father's son. If he'd inherited his father's predisposition to flit from one woman to another, he'd also inherited the looks and charm that made him irresistible to women.

And there were glimpses of her attraction to him. He hadn't been mistaken—her cheeks had pinkened when he'd held her hand a moment earlier.

So what gives?

"Have I forgotten about another date?" Hilary asked.

"No. I'm here to sweep you away to a picnic area my family owns. I'm sure you've heard of my family's citrus grove. It's beautiful right now." He gave her his most charming grin. *I'll thaw that heart of hers yet.*

She hesitated, as if weighing two untenable options. He sensed Jo making a shooing motion behind him and pressed his lips together to stifle a laugh. Finally, Hilary said, "Sure. Let's go." She said bye to Jo, who waved both of them off.

"Your enthusiasm is killing me." Outside Jo's condo, he opened the door to his Bugatti.

She flushed. "Sorry. I'm a little tired from last night. Didn't get much sleep."

"Really?" He gave her an expression of mock disbelief. "How could that be? You went home alone."

She laughed half-heartedly as he started off. "How did you know where to find me?"

"Wasn't that hard. I stopped by your place, and a woman who looked a lot like you said you were at Josephine's." He glanced over. "Gavin never mentioned that you had a sister."

"Bebe's more of an…estranged cousin." Hilary shifted in her seat. "You talk with her long?"

"Not really. Why?"

"Did she say or, um, do anything else?"

"No. Not particularly." There was no point in talking about how Bebe had shamelessly displayed her assets. Embarrassing relatives were a mood killer, and not something he wanted Hilary to think about.

She crossed her arms and looked out at the passing scenery. He put on some soft music and continued driving. She probably didn't believe him about Bebe's behavior, but she would forget all about it once she arrived at the grove. It was the Pryce family's pride and joy, and everyone loved it there.

PEOPLE DIDN'T EXAGGERATE WHEN THEY SPOKE OF how magnificent the Pryce grove was. The driveway led to a spacious parking area surrounded by lime trees. A gigantic three-story house made of bone-white stone overlooked the grove. Mark explained that most of the family's cooking took place in the manse's enormous kitchen, although the picnic barbecuing was done out in a field surrounded by orange trees. Then he picked up a basket from a waiting staff member and led her around the house, toward the actual grove.

Rows and rows of orange trees lined the fertile field. Sun-bleached bricks formed a flat and even path that connected the house to the picnic area in the center, near a man-made lake. The lake was something else altogether, with a carefully designed water garden that was encircled by roughly hewn stone blocks. Ducks and fish shared the tranquil water with lilies that looked like something Monet would have painted. The scents of citrus, soil and flowers mingled in the air, and it was almost too heady to breathe it all in.

Somebody had already spread a red- and white-checked picnic blanket under a tree. Mark placed the basket on it.

"Wow," Hilary whispered as she sat down.

"Pretty nice, huh?"

"I'd heard a lot about it, but this… This is gorgeous."

"Pride of the family."

"I heard your mother and father both spend a lot of time here."

A shadow crossed his eyes. It hinted at some old pain, and the possibility surprised her. She'd always assumed he'd lived a great life. After all, he was Mark Pryce, who'd never failed at anything and had all the success and women and everything else a man could hope for. Before she could ponder it more, a bright smile lit his face. "Yeah, but not to farm in case you're wondering," he said in a cheery tone.

Maybe she'd imagined the earlier look. "Then why have so many orange trees?"

"Our great-great-great-grandfather married a citrus farmer's daughter. She started it as a hobby." He pulled out a bucket of fried chicken and another of mashed potatoes from the basket.

"I had no idea you ate fried chicken," she said.

"Why wouldn't I?"

"You just seem more like an *haute cuisine* type. I figured you'd have foie gras and slow roasted duck glazed with, I don't know, a port reduction or something like that."

He laughed. "I do slum here and there. Even eat the occasional donut."

"You don't say. And do your fancy chefs know about this?"

"Absolutely not. They'd have my head."

The chicken was excellent, juicy and tender inside, and crispy and spicy outside. And whoever had made the mashed potatoes and gravy was a kitchen god. If this was culinary slumming, she could slum for the rest of her life. Mark poured her a glass of cool white wine, which turned out to be both fruity and crisp. He definitely hadn't slummed on the drink choice. Hilary recognized the label— she'd seen it on the wine menu at La Mer.

They talked about this and that, about acquaintances and where they wanted to go. "Some place fun and far away," she said. "I've never traveled overseas. I want to go to Europe one day."

"We should go together."

She gave him a quick smile. She doubted they'd have the time to go any time soon, and that meant she would never go with him. Still, she didn't want to ruin the moment by pointing that out. It was sweet of him to offer.

Once she was full, she lay on the blanket with her eyes closed. The branches provided a rustling green canopy, and she enjoyed the breeze and the gentle sound of the ducks and the feel of Mark's body so close to hers. He wasn't quite touching her, and she wanted him to slide those last few inches toward her. It was dangerous—oh so crazy dangerous—but for a few minutes she wanted to pretend she wasn't a Rosenberg girl.

Then she felt it—him wrapping a lock of her hair around his finger and toying with it. She opened her eyes. What woman could resist those gorgeous blues or the small bemused smile that tugged at the corners of his sensual lips? And if she didn't like blue, there were always his bright intelligence, humor and passion.

Their eyes locked, and the world seemed to suddenly go into slow motion. She felt like she was floating, pulled into the seductive haze he was creating with his gaze moving between her lips and eyes.

"Kiss me, Hilary," he whispered.

And she did. She wanted to know what it was like to taste him. He didn't take over at the first touch of her lips on his. He let her lead, as though telling her she was the one in charge. She could go as far as she wanted, and he'd follow.

She traced his mouth with the tip of her tongue, enjoying the masculine texture and taste of him. It was better than her fantasy. He still didn't open up, so she probed gently, letting him know she wanted it too. His heart thundered under her palm, and a sweet ache she hadn't felt in years knotted in her belly.

His tongue finally tangled with hers, and she moaned, tightening her hold on him. He was still braced over her, his arm muscles solid and tight. She wrapped her hand around his broad shoulders and tried to pull him closer, but he didn't budge. So she clung to him, kissing him like this was the last kiss she'd ever have.

She could never repeat a kiss that inspired so many conflicting emotions in her. She was dying for more, but at the same time scared of what might happen if she gave in to the passion and let go. She could enjoy it for now, since things were still light and casual between them. But she needed to pull back before it sucked her in and drowned her. Down that path lay the wrecked lives of the women in her family.

When she lessened the pressure and started to let go, Mark growled softly, wrapped his arms around her and rolled so that she was on top of him. His strong, large hand buried deep in her hair, he pulled her down for an open-mouthed kiss, full of tongues and desperate needs and desire.

Hilary might have been able to push away earlier, but no longer, not when she'd glimpsed Mark's stark passion. It was like a drug, flooding her body and clouding her mind. All she could do was feel the headiness and the way her limbs grew heavy and languid under his sensual assault. The sharpest yet sweetest ache she'd ever known spread from her heart in waves, and she wanted him more than anything. She would—

He moved until she straddled him, cradling his thick, hard length between her legs. She rocked against him, her eyes on his. He groaned, and she reached for his shorts, ready to rip them off him.

A sudden quacking on the pond jerked her out of the sensual haze. She flinched and dropped her hands. The idea that they'd been so close to losing control stopped her.

This… This wasn't like her. The woman she was trying to be wouldn't be rolling around in an open field where anybody could be watching…or walk by at any moment. And the woman she was trying to be certainly wouldn't be doing it with a man with a reputation for loving-and-leaving in three months. Even Tim had stuck around longer than that.

Suddenly cold with fear and self-recrimination, she pushed off him. He let go and watched her, his eyes dark and unreadable. Her hands shook as she tidied her hair. She'd lost her scrunchy—it was probably under Mark, but she didn't want to stick around to find it. "I…" she began, then swallowed miserably. What was there to say? How could she explain how screwed up she was?

What had Bebe said the night before? *We're all the fucking same.*

Hilary closed her eyes. She couldn't accept that. She couldn't be like her mom and aunt and Bebe. "I'm sorry," she said then fled toward the house.

SHIT. WHAT THE HELL JUST HAPPENED?

Mark sat up and watched Hilary vanish. Women didn't run after he kissed them. They clung to him and rocked against him and ripped his clothes off.

A part of him wanted to go after her. But then what? It'd get heavy and serious, wouldn't it? Then what would he do? Act like it was all still easy and fun after he'd run after her like an idiot?

"Good god, was that Gavin's secretary?"

Mark jerked his head upward at his father's incredulous voice. "When did you get here?" he asked sharply.

"Just a moment ago. I was going over some details of the party with the groundskeeper. I heard you were seeing her, but I thought it was a joke."

"You weren't at the concert last night," Mark said, suddenly realizing he hadn't seen his dad there.

"Something came up at the last minute, and I had to cancel. Eliza doesn't mind so long as she gets my money." Salazar sat down on the blanket and folded his long frame so that he wouldn't wrinkle his suit. He was one of the few people—other than lawyers and accountants—who wore suits in L.A. "She's not your type, you know."

This was getting old. "You don't know what my type is."

"Of course I do. Young blondes with boob jobs. Everyone knows this."

"Am I really that obvious?"

Salazar shrugged. "You're young and having fun."

"Am I?"

"Aren't you?"

Mark didn't answer.

"If it's not fun, why do it?" Salazar asked.

Mark mulled that over. "Is it fun for you?"

A small muscle in Salazar's cheek ticked. "It's what I am, Mark."

"Bullshit."

"We all have our flaws. We can't change just because we want to. It doesn't work that way." Salazar sighed. "If it did, we'd do everything we put our minds to. No matter how much I will it, I'll never climb Mount Everest."

"Is that why you didn't divorce Mom to be with *her?*"

Salazar started. But cool indifference quickly masked his face.

"You cared a great deal for Georgia Love, didn't you?" Mark said.

"What makes you say that?"

"You flinched. And you gave Blaine fifty million," Mark said, referring to the son his father had had with that other woman. Georgia Love Davis was the only one Salazar had looked up from time to time. She must've been special. Salazar wasn't the type to reminisce about his exes. There were too many to give a damn about.

"I did care for her, but she wasn't like most women I dated. She could've forgiven all my flaws except my inability to stay faithful. It would've wounded her too gravely. I couldn't do it."

Mark felt something bitter and poisonous unfurling inside him. It ran its claws along the old and ugly memories that he'd sworn never to remember again. "But you could do it to Mom."

"Your mother knew what she was getting into," Salazar said, his voice without inflection. "She still chose to marry me, even after having read the prenup. Her lawyer reviewed it, so I'm quite certain she understood exactly what it meant."

"She gave you five children."

"That too was her choice. I never asked her for so many. I only wanted one son."

"Yes. Dane, who doesn't give a damn about anybody. Sort of like you in a way."

"Mark." There was a sharp warning in Salazar's voice.

"Do you give a shit about anybody but yourself?" Mark rose and glared down at his father, who remained seated. "Have you ever wondered why she had five children with you?"

"Yes, I have." Salazar's voice gained in volume and intensity. "She wanted to use them—use *you*—to control me. It's not my fault she thought wrong. We can't always change who we are. That's why we live the lives we live."

"That's not true," Mark said. "Mom's changed. She used to smile a lot, spend time with all of us. Now she doesn't. Something's snapped, and she rarely smiles, and she rarely spends time with any of us."

"Perhaps she'd smile more if you agreed to date the heiress she picked out for you. Have you considered that?" Salazar gave him a pitying look. "You think dating Hilary is going to prove...what? That you aren't what people say you are? That you can be in a relationship for more than three months? That you're so much better than me because you can *change*?"

His words hit like a physical blow, and Mark listened, his spine rigid.

"Don't be a judgmental idiot. Whatever you're doing with Hilary will end in three months or less. Then you'll be back to dating your young big-chested blondes because that's who you are, what you like." Salazar stood, his motion fluid and elegant. "Do you think your mother's a blameless saint in all this? I know about her lovers. But I'm willing to look the other way for the sake of the family. I hope you're old enough to understand." He adjusted his cuff links and walked away, leaving Mark stunned.

How could Salazar know about the men? Mark knew…but only because he'd inadvertently walked in on one of them when he'd been nine. His mother hadn't realized and neither had her lover, but Mark had figured out that she was doing what Dad was doing to her.

And unlike Salazar, Ceinlys hadn't done it to kill time. She'd done it to seek comfort and solace because she couldn't get either from her husband.

Not when giving him five children hadn't been enough to change him.

Slowly, Mark made his way to the house. Hilary stood in the foyer, hugging herself. She was pale, and her eyes were red like she was on the verge of breaking down.

This was what he'd done to her by kissing her.

He wanted to show everyone they were wrong about him. He wasn't an asshole who didn't deserve the love of a good woman because he couldn't stay put for more than three months. But he couldn't use Hilary as his guinea pig. If his father was right about him and he couldn't change, he'd only end up hurting her.

A woman who wasn't loved the way she deserved to be loved would warp and harden and become bitter. He'd seen it happen with his mother. The slow poisoning of a life.

Hilary deserved better.

"Hey—" she began at the same time he said, "I—"

Mark cleared his throat. "Go ahead."

"Yeah. Well. I should get going now. I have a ton of work to do," she said lamely.

"Okay." He shoved his hands into his pockets and fisted them tightly.

"I'm probably going to be very busy in the next several days. You know how it is."

"Sure."

"I'll have the clothes, shoes and everything messengered to you as soon as possible."

"It's okay. I'll send somebody to pick them up."

"No, really. I don't mind."

Damn it. This was what their conversation had been reduced to? This horrible awkward stiffness? "Okay. I'll drop you off at Jo's so you can get your car."

"That'd be great. Thanks."

"Yeah. No problem." He managed a smile even though what he really wanted to do was punch the stone wall of the house until his hands bled.

But even that pain wouldn't be enough to blot out the bitter misery in his heart.

TWELVE

OVER THE NEXT FEW DAYS THERE WAS NO word from Mark. Hilary told herself this was exactly what she wanted until the Pryce family party on the Fourth. Still, every time she walked into her office and saw an empty desk, she felt a twinge of disappointment.

How stupid.

The more affectionate and sweet he was, the worse it would be for her. Given his reputation, people were already calling her a Quarterly Girl. Did she want to make it harder by actually feeling something for him?

Except she was afraid it might be too late. He made her feel so alive and special just by being near her and looking at her in that way that said she was the center of his universe. She knew she wasn't—he'd probably done that with every one of his Quarterly Girls—but her heart didn't care.

Thankfully, the picnic hadn't been a total disaster. She hadn't let the kiss go too far. She wasn't like her mother and aunt, who would do anything to please a man in their lives. Hilary pleased and took care of herself first. Counting on a man to do so would be a monumental mistake.

On the fifth day of radio silence, Gavin looked up as he finished dictating instructions. "Are you all right?" he asked. "You look really pale."

"I'm fine," she managed to say in a normal voice, despite the scratchy and sore throat. She smiled for his benefit. "Didn't get much sleep last night is all. In fact, I was just about to get more coffee. Want some?"

He shook his head. "I hope you get better sleep tonight."

"Thanks." Hilary went to the break room and got her fifth coffee of the day. She didn't even have much appetite—her stomach felt too unsettled for anything solid, and nights were spent mostly tossing and turning.

She started back toward her office and swayed. Little black and gray dots appeared in her vision, and she blinked rapidly, one hand on the wall for support.

"Hey, you all right?" Sally said, trotting toward her.

"Fine." Hilary looked down and saw coffee on both the floor and her shoes. "Crap. I made a mess. Sorry." She grabbed a fistful of paper towels to mop it up. Then she promptly lost her balance and lurched forward.

"Oh my god!" Sally's voice sounded distant for some reason. "Hilary!"

Hilary sensed people converging around her. What was going on? Why did she feel so confused? The gears in her head turned like they were covered with sticky glue.

She felt a strong masculine hand on her shoulder. "Hilary, are you all right? You need to go to the hospital or something?"

"No, it's okay." She blinked up at Gavin. "I'm sorry, it's just me being clumsy. Did I trip and fall?"

"No, you fainted." His face took on the look that said he'd just made up his mind to do something. "I'm having Thomas drive you to the hospital." He pulled out his phone.

"No!" Thomas was Gavin's trusted chauffeur. Her boss never went anywhere without Thomas driving him, and she couldn't take him.

"Yes. And you're going to stay put," Gavin ordered, then spoke rapidly into the phone.

Hilary managed to sit up with Sally's help and said, "There's no need to make a big deal about this. I just need to go home and get some rest, that's all. Just call me a cab, please?"

"No. Thomas's going to drive you and make sure you get home safely. It's non-negotiable." Gavin frowned. "You should've called in sick if you didn't feel well."

"But I never call in sick."

"First time for everything, Hilary. And don't come in tomorrow."

"Why not?" she said, half-panicked.

"Because you're sick and it's Saturday. Stay home and recuperate. I'm being a terrible boss for even saying this, but I do need you healthy by next week"

She exhaled softly while looking up at her boss's concerned face. "You do?"

"Yes. How am I going to function without you?" He gave her a small smile. "Now, go get some rest and recuperate. That's an order."

BEBE FINISHED THE CHEAPEST BURGER MICKEY D'S offered and washed it down with the dregs of her soft drink. She couldn't believe Hilary had split the day after she'd come home. How the hell could her cousin do that? Did she think she was too good to share the same roof?

Bitch.

God, Bebe couldn't stand what Hilary had become. She used to be so much fun, drinking, hanging out and smoking pot. Now she was this straight-laced boring ass suit who went to work and kissed her boss's butt every day so he wouldn't fire her. She wasn't holding down her job because of her smarts, that was for sure. She'd been a C student in high school, and she hadn't done that great in college either. What was that boring shit she'd studied? Women's literature or something?

So pretentious.

Hilary didn't have to be so self-righteous and smug about the fact that she had a fancy job. Her cousin probably held on to it by blowing her boss every morning or something. Freddie had told her Hilary had mad oral skills.

The girl could be less uptight and more fun.

And Bebe's reappearance in her life should've reminded Hilary how much fun they could have together if she'd just loosen back up. But nooooo. She wouldn't even return Bebe's calls about Mr. Dark and Handsome. And rich too from the looks of it. She'd made a note of the car Mark drove. Bugattis were expensive.

Greedy, greedy, greedy.

Hilary probably thought she could cut Bebe out of it. She always tried to deny where she came from—how they were all the same. It didn't matter what Hilary wore or where she worked. She was still a Rosenberg girl, and Rosenberg girls laughed easy, fucked easier and didn't care about anything except living as large as possible in the moment.

Just 'cuz Bebe didn't go to some college didn't

mean she didn't know how to use Google. She'd already found out who the guy was, where he worked and how much money he had.

Two billion and change. Hilary had done well for herself.

It was time she shared.

MARK SIGHED, LOOKING AT THE EMPTY RESTAU-rant from behind the bar counter. La Mer had just cleared its massive lunch crowd, who'd collectively dropped an ungodly sum on the best seafood the city had to offer.

He should be proud and happy about the con-tinued success, but instead he was tired and restless. His hand closed around his phone. He wanted to call Hilary and see how she was doing, but some-thing made him hesitate. She might be happier without him pestering her.

In the last five days, he'd been running an experiment to put his father's theory to the test. Granted, it hadn't even been four weeks since he'd asked Hilary out, but if he was really like his father, somebody else should've snagged his interest by now…right?

But it didn't matter how many trendy clubs and bars he hit with Iain or how many young, receptive blondes he'd run into. The only woman he could think about was Hilary.

So what did that mean?

Larry, the maître d', came toward him at a rapid pace, his face dark. "There's somebody here to see you," he said in a clipped voice.

"Who?"

"I don't know. I've never seen a woman like her before. I tried to get rid of her, but she insisted you would see her."

Huh. Strange. If Larry didn't recognize her, it couldn't be one of his exes or family or friends. Was it the heiress? What was her name again…? Oh yeah, Katarina.

"If you want, I can call the cops," Larry offered.

"It's all right." If it was Katarina, calling cops on her would embarrass his mother. "I'll see her."

To his surprise it was Hilary's cousin at the entrance. It took a moment to recall that her name was Bebe. Her hair was stylishly curled, but she wore a cheap white cotton shirt—again overly thin and without any bra underneath—and ripped denim shorts. It was a miracle Larry hadn't called the cops without bothering Mark first. Her strappy sandals tokked on the marbled floor as she turned. Her makeup was dark and laid on a bit too thick. It had a cheap chalkiness that highlighted her wrinkles.

"Hey, you," she said with a smile.

"What can I do for you?" He kept his tone just polite enough to be discouraging without being rude. She was Hilary's cousin, after all.

Something sharp and scornful flashed through her eyes, but it disappeared as she smiled even more broadly. "I was wondering what you're doing with my cousin."

"That's…really none of your business." He didn't trust a woman who showed more teeth than warmth when she smiled.

"It *is* my business." She moved closer to him. "Look, I know all there is to know about Hilary, okay? We grew up together. And I know what you want—Hilary. But given the kind of guy you are, you're probably doing everything wrong."

Mark regarded the woman. It was true; he didn't know that much about Hilary. She rarely talked about personal stuff—her history, her childhood—and he hadn't probed. What was so important that Bebe had to share? His gut told him it wasn't anything good, but he wanted to know. Knowledge was power, even if it was just petty gossip. And hearing what Bebe had to say might shed some light on what had hurt Hilary at Eliza's event. "All right. Come to my office."

Bebe smiled and followed him back through the restaurant. Mark felt his staff's curious gazes and ignored them. The people who worked at La Mer were discreet, and they wouldn't blab about a poorly dressed woman going into his office.

He left the door open and sat behind his desk. She took an empty chair without any prompting from him and crossed her legs. "Look, I don't know what you think you're doing," she began, "but you're dating a Rosenberg girl. You don't do roses, evening gowns and things."

"Really?" he drawled.

"We're a family of wild women doing wild things." She uncrossed her legs and leaned forward. "Did she tell you about us?"

"No."

Bebe smirked. "How silly of her. We're sort of like half-sisters slash cousins. Know what I'm sayin'?"

"No. And if you don't get to the point in the next five seconds, I'm throwing you out." He didn't have the patience for whatever game she wanted to play.

She smirked. "My mom and her mom were identical twins. And at one point, they were doing the same guy. Hilary and I were born on the same day and we have the same father."

A sudden coldness coiled in his belly. "You have the same father and you were born on the same day?" What the hell. And he thought *his* parents had a messed-up marriage. "So your father was cheating on your mom with—"

NADIA LEE

Bebe's expression changed to one of intense concern. "Oh no. Oh my gosh, sorry if I gave you that impression. No, I mean...my mom and aunt—Hilary's mom—*shared* him." She tilted her head. "Do you understand?"

Mark's mind blanked out for a moment. She couldn't possibly be saying what he thought she was saying.

"Yes, Mark. They were in a ménage." She leaned back comfortably. "And that's how Hilary and I grew up, watching our mothers and our father. When he got tired of us, he'd take off for a bit, then come back when he missed us. It was our normal everyday life."

Normal? There was nothing normal about what she was saying.

She shifted. "Hilary and I would've had one ourselves, too...until she chickened out at the last minute."

Hilary? In a threesome with her half-sister/cousin? He couldn't wrap his mind around that at all.

"Giving her fancy dresses and stuff? You're not going to land her in bed that way. You don't treat a Rosenberg girl like a princess. You treat her the way she understands, does that make sense?"

"And that would be...?"

"What she's seen growing up! Man, for a rich guy you're not too quick." Bebe shook her head. "She doesn't understand anything else. Why do you think she broke up with her doctor?"

"He cheated on her."

"Is that what she told you?" Bebe convulsed with laughter. Wiping tears from her eyes, she said, "You're so naïve."

There was nothing funny about the way that doctor had hurt Hilary, and Bebe was seriously starting to grate on his nerves. "She didn't have to tell me," Mark snapped. "I was there."

Abruptly, Bebe stopped laughing and shrugged. "Forget it. It's something you should ask her. I don't feel comfortable spilling her secrets."

He clenched his hands. He didn't generally feel violent, but he was getting pretty close. "The way she grew up? How to get her into bed? Those aren't secrets?"

"Everyone knows, Mark. Her boyfriend in college—the one we could've had together—knew. That's why he wanted to date her, and that's why she'd fallen for him, until she got stupid and greedy about it and didn't want to share. You know she got all huffy when it was her time to commit to it? Acted like we were beneath her? But look at her." Bebe sneered. "Still living with my mom. Why would she do that if she's so much better than the rest of us?

"She's just a Rosenberg girl. And whether she admits it to herself or not, subconsciously she's looking for a guy who'll remind her of that fact. So be that guy if you want her. You get it now?"

She pulled out a piece of paper from her shorts and slapped it on the desk. "She's not answering her phone, and she's not home. So after you're done thinkin' things through, you call me, and we'll figure out an arrangement that makes us all happy." She stood up and gave him an arch look. "Who knows? If you play your cards right, you might just get two for the price of one."

THIRTEEN

WHAT THE HELL? HAD SHE JUST PROPO-
sitioned him?

Mark watched Bebe walk away, the shorts swinging saucily. Larry would make sure she exited the restaurant.

Leaning back in his seat, Mark took a pencil and drummed out a rapid staccato on the armrest with the eraser. He didn't believe for a second she'd come to offer him helpful advice. She wanted a piece of him, but probably knew she had no chance. She didn't seem stupid. Vipers like her often weren't. So she thought to use Hilary, except he wasn't dumb enough fall for her little game.

He pieced together all the things she'd said… and the ones she'd omitted. It was obvious Hilary's father had been a jackass. Bebe might have called her parents' relationship a ménage, like it was some kind of hip new lifestyle, but he bet it hadn't been like that for Hilary.

No wonder she'd been so wary. He remembered how she'd rejected him in the owm lobby and run off after the ugly confrontation with that doctor's fiancée. The situation had most likely served as a reminder of her messed up past.

Then there was his reputation.

He winced, thinking about all the "Quarterly Girls." His college buddies had come up with that. They'd even patted themselves on the back for being so clever, but Mark bet Hilary didn't share their sentiment. She probably thought Mark too would be like her lowlife dad who never committed to any woman and flitted in and out of their lives. It was a pretty sure bet that her dad hadn't abstained while he was away.

Damn. Mark had assumed wrong. He'd thought he was starting at zero with her. But in reality, he'd been starting at something like negative two thousand. There were so many things stacked against him. Not calling her after the picnic at the grove…

She'd had to have been testing him to see how he measured up compared to her dad or that asshole boyfriend she'd had in college…or her two-timing doc. And Mark had failed spectacularly by pulling back—that had been easier after the uncomfortable conversation with his dad.

He was such an idiot.

Cursing, he left La Mer and drove straight to Hilary's office. At her desk was Sally.

"Hello, Mark," she said with a smile that was bordering on confused. "Have an appointment with Gavin?"

"No. Where's Hilary?"

"She went home." She frowned. "Is something wrong?"

"Why did she go home?" It was barely three thirty, and no one in Gavin's firm ever went home early, much less his right hand woman.

"Didn't you hear? She was really sick." Sally placed an elbow on the desk and rested her chin on the back of her hand. "She was really pale. I think she might've even passed out."

A small ball of panic rolled through him. "Why didn't she go to the hospital?"

"She insisted. So Gavin had Thomas drive her home."

He swore. It had to be pretty serious for Gavin to let his chauffeur take her home. Gavin never drove in L.A. traffic.

Bebe had said Hilary wasn't home. So the small house was out of the question. "Is Gavin available?"

Sally shook her head. "He's in a meeting."

"How about Thomas? Do you know how to get ahold of him?"

"Sure." She dialed a number and handed him the receiver.

Thomas understood the situation—for a man who did nothing except drive Gavin's fancy cars he was remarkably well plugged-in—and he told Mark that Hilary was staying at Josephine Martinez's condo. Did Mark need directions too?

Mark told him that wasn't necessary and went over to Josephine's place. Every time the light turned red, he felt like a thirsty man just a few feet away from an oasis. Hilary was probably home alone—Josephine was far too busy to play nurse—and based on what Sally had said, Hilary definitely needed somebody to watch over her. What if she tried to get something…like water…and passed out and hit her head against a table or something? Who would be there to call an ambulance and make sure she was all right?

The uniformed doorman at the condo was the same one who'd been here the week before. He recognized Mark instantly. "Sorry, Mr. Pryce. I'll need to call Ms. Martinez's unit first," he said, shrugging his skinny shoulders apologetically. "You aren't on the list."

"Are you kidding?"

"Uh…"

Mark sighed impatiently. "Do I look like a psycho stalker killer to you?"

The doorman bit his lower lip. "No, but…"

"You know I've been here before." Shaking his

head, Mark signed in for Josephine's unit. "Call ahead if you want. Just don't try to stop me."

Leaving the uncertain doorman behind, Mark took the elevator, which seemed to go up at a sloth's pace. Damn it. He should just buy Hilary a penthouse unit next to his or something. This was getting ridiculous.

When he finally reached Jo's door and knocked, no one answered. Was Hilary too sick to get up? Had she managed to hurt herself, like in his imaginary scenario? Mark paced the corridor a bit, feeling impotent, then thought to try the door handle.

The door opened.

He felt a small measure of relief, then scowled. *Hilary should be locking her door.* The building had its own doorman and security, but that wasn't a good enough reason to be careless with her safety. He finally understood why Gavin always seemed to want to hire an army of bodyguards for his family… because he was feeling the same compulsion right now.

"Hello? Anyone home?" he said in a low voice. No answer. The condo was stark with very few prints on the white walls. Some would call the design minimalist, but Mark thought the place lacked something. It just looked sterile.

He crossed the hardwood floor, trying to step quietly, and reached the end of the hall. One of the rooms had its door ajar. He peeked through and saw Hilary curled up on her side on the bed. Her blouse and skirt stretched over her curved back, and she wasn't moving.

Was she asleep?

He tiptoed inside and looked at her. One hand was pressed against her belly; she looked so small and helpless, adjectives he'd never thought to associate with her. She'd always appeared formidable, thoroughly competent and strong. Her skin felt cool under his, and he rummaged around the condo until he found a spare blanket and draped it over her. She barely stirred.

Sitting on the edge of a chair near her bed, he watched her rest. He'd never played nurse before. But he knew how it was done—he remembered his mother sitting with him when he'd been sick. She'd held his hand, smoothed the sweat from his forehead and whispered sweet nothings…sometimes even hummed to comfort him. Despite all the nannies Salazar had hired, Ceinlys had always taken care of her children personally when they weren't feeling well.

Would Hilary find it comforting if he took her hand and whispered sweet nothings, or would she be horrified? He could never predict how she'd react to him.

But there was one thing she always reacted to

rather predictably. So he pulled out his phone and dialed.

HILARY KEPT HER EYES CLOSED. HER HEAD FELT like it was submerged in syrup. What the heck had happened at the office? Now that her brain started to kick in a bit, she cringed. God, she'd almost fainted.

How embarrassing.

So what if she'd been under a lot of pressure and stress? The two went hand-in-hand. It wasn't like she didn't know what working for Gavin required. It was her job to ensure she was indispensable to her boss. If he asked her to pluck the stars from the sky, then pluck the stars she would.

She should shower and get something to eat. She really needed to go back to work the next day even if Gavin fussed about it. This wasn't like her. She'd never called in sick.

She sighed, cranked her eyes open and immediately yelped. Her hand flew to her chest. "Oh my gosh, Mark! What are you doing here?"

"Hey." He gave her a small grin. "Heard you were sick, so I figured I'd check up on you."

"How long have you been sitting there?"

He shrugged. "I don't know. A few hours? I wasn't really counting."

"Oh…" He didn't have anything in his hands. "Were you…watching me the whole time?"

"I might have dozed off a bit here and there." He gave her an unexpectedly sheepish smile, and she had to press her hand hard against her chest to stop a pang. She hoped it was from her unusual condition, nothing more. Because if it was from Mark's smile…

She was in the biggest trouble of her life.

"Do you want to eat something?" he asked. "I've got some soup I can heat up."

"You? Soup?" She blinked. "I thought you only did haute cuisine…unless you're slumming."

He laughed. "No. I had the La Mer chef whip it up. He wasn't thrilled with my chicken noodle soup order."

"So it's going to be either really good or really bad?"

"Knowing him, probably really good. I told him it was for a beautiful woman who was too sick to eat anything else."

She swallowed. He really needed to stop saying stuff like that…and especially stop looking at her like he meant it. She shuddered to think what her appearance must be right now. *Absolutely awful.* But somehow, under his sweet gaze, she felt like she was the loveliest woman in the world. Was this some kind of power men had over women? Was this why her mother hadn't been able to wean herself from

Tim, no matter how toxic he was? If Hilary wasn't careful, she could get addicted to Mark, even knowing they would go their separate ways after his family party.

She started to rise, but he put out a hand to stop her. "Hey, patient, you stay put. I'll bring you your soup." He started to move toward the door, walking backwards and keeping his eyes on her. "Don't even think about getting up. I mean it!" He gave her one last mock scowl and vanished into the hall.

She pulled her legs up and hugged them while he clanged around in the kitchen. This was a new experience. People didn't take care of her when she was sick. Tim had hated being near sick kids. "They're gonna gimme their germs and shit," he'd say and take off for days. Hilary's mom and aunt hadn't been very good at nursing either, basically just checking up on her every so often to make sure she wasn't dead. But when one of them had been sick, it had been up to her to do something about it. And she'd done what she could, which had never been enough. Bebe had started running off as soon as she'd hit her teens. "I'm not getting your disease. Have fun recovering," she'd say before taking off.

The door opened, and Mark came in carrying a tray that had a bowl of steaming soup and a piece of thick crusty bread. "Courtesy of La Mer catering," he announced gravely, as though he were a butler.

She sat up, already feeling better. "I had no idea you were branching out."

"It's a secret. I don't want Luc to kill me. I'm pretty sure he knows how to make poison."

"Afraid he might slip a little into your fish?" She took a spoonful of the soup and closed her eyes at the sublime flavor. "This is *the* chicken noodle soup. My god, it's divine."

"Great. So I don't have to look for a new chef?"

She chuckled. "You do not. And thank you. This is really lovely."

"Well, somebody's gotta take care of you. Look at you, here all alone." He gestured around. "What's the point of a best friend roommate if she's not here to play Florence Nightingale?"

"I think she has to make money to pay for the condo."

"Ppffftt."

"If she doesn't work, she doesn't get paid."

"Kind of like me. If I don't work, I don't get laid."

She snorted. "I highly doubt that." She finished the soup and leaned back against the headboard. "Um, I was thinking…"

"Yeah?"

"You basically need a date to avoid dating whoever your mother picked out, right?"

Crossing his arms, he regarded her. "Riiiight."

She cleared her throat. Why was this so hard? She'd spent hours on research, making sure the list would be eminently suitable. "Anyway, I think if that's what you really want, you shouldn't go with me. Your mother will never believe we're dating."

A harsh frown snapped onto his face. "Hey, we were seen at Eliza's event."

"That's irrelevant." People had seen through her there. Mark might have been oblivious then, with so many guests milling around and distracting him, but he'd notice when the setting was smaller and more intimate. "You need a woman who's, you know, someone that somebody like you would date."

"Really. For example?"

"Meredith Lloyd—"

He choked. "Gavin's baby sister? Are you serious?"

She continued, undeterred. "Beatrice Sterling." Beatrice was from an impeccable family, superbly wealthy too. There was nothing to nitpick about the Sterlings.

"Under the thumb of that horrible autocratic curmudgeon? No thanks."

"Isabelle Hall."

"Not marrying into a political family. That'd be worse than Barron Sterling."

"Well, there—"

"Forget it, Hilary." He swatted her suggestions

away. "I'm not going with anybody but you. If you back out now, I won't be able to avoid that woman Mom picked out."

Her mouth formed an O. "Really?"

"Yeah. Look, I want to take you to the party. You, not some other woman. Why is that so hard to believe?"

Mutely she stared at him. No man had ever wanted just her. No man had ever made her want to believe what he felt for her was true.

His expression slowly turned into an unreadable mask. "Let's cut to the chase, Hilary. If you don't want to go with me, just say so. Forget about owing me a favor. People are going to know if I bring a date who'd rather be somewhere else."

That's not your problem. Say no, the smarter part of her urged, but somehow she couldn't do it. "Okay," she said finally. "I'll go."

"And this has nothing to do with that Morrigan's thing."

"No."

His shoulders relaxed. He put the tray off on the side and leaned in until their lips were almost touching. She pulled back, eyes wide.

"You're going to get whatever I have," she whispered.

His gaze dropped briefly to her mouth. "I don't care."

"You will when you get sick."

"Then we'll C and R."

"What?" she said shakily, unable to keep her gaze from darting between his eyes and his lips.

"Cuddle and Recuperate." He gave her a wink that was breathtakingly sexy. "Now shut up and kiss me, woman."

FOURTEEN

HILARY PRESSED HER WARM, MOIST MOUTH against his, and he almost groaned at how much he'd missed her. He couldn't quite believe she'd said yes. He'd been sure she would pull away like she always did. It was crazy how victorious and invincible that one simple word made him feel. Countless women had said it before, but it had never had the same effect.

There was so much shyness in the touch, as though they'd never kissed before.

Or maybe it was him who kissed like he'd never done it. All the other women crumbled in his memory like pillars of salt. All he cared about was Hilary.

And with the sense of elation came a sense of responsibility—he could never hurt her. Having her in his arms like this was a privilege that made his heart sing. She made him hopeful for things he'd never dared hope for.

Her tongue brushed against his as she tightened her grip around his shoulders, and all his thoughts scattered. All he could focus on was this gorgeous woman in his arms who was melting against him the way he'd fantasized for weeks…months…maybe even longer.

He cupped her curvy butt in his hand, pulling her closer.

He had no idea what it was about Hilary that made him want to be so careful around her. There was a part of him that said he'd only get one chance to make anything of this, and that any wrong move would screw it up for him and hurt her. He ran his hand along her smooth curves and groaned. Damn, she made him so hard with those sexy noises in her throat. He wanted to take this as far as they could go…have her fall apart in his arms…until he remembered the soup tray that was lying next to her.

Shit. What kind of a jerk seduced a woman when she was sick?

Reluctantly he pulled back. There was a question in her eyes.

"Hey." He kissed her on the forehead. "No hanky-panky when you're sick. Get some rest, sweetheart."

She sighed. "I should've known you'd say that."

"You should have?"

"Despite your reputation, you're a pretty good

guy." She gave him a lopsided smile. "But if you tell anybody I said so, I'll deny it."

"Okay. It'll just be our secret."

It wasn't like anybody would believe it anyway. He wasn't the nicest guy when it came to women. There were reasons why his exes were called Quarterly Girls. And as much as he'd like to blame them for becoming boring, he couldn't help but wonder—after all, he was the only common point in those failed relationships. Many of them had gone on to date the same guy much longer than three months. A few had even gotten married.

He took the tray to the kitchen and loaded the dishwasher. Keys rattled at the door, and Josephine walked in. She looked fashionable as usual in a sleeveless red Dior and stilettos. A loopy two-tone metal belt cinched her small waist, and her hair was flung over one shoulder. "Oh, you're still here. The doorman said you'd come in. What's up?"

"Heard Hilary's sick, so I came by to see how she's doing."

"Looks like it's more than that." She sniffed. "Did you cook something?"

He laughed. "I don't cook. I employ cooks."

"Huh." Giving him an assessing look, she dumped her purse and shopping bags on the couch. He'd never seen her without at least one glossy bag from some boutique shop in the city. "Why are you really here?"

"I just told you."

"Yeah, but if you'd just wanted to know how she's doing, you could've called. There wasn't any reason for you to actually come over, much less bring food. And from the smell of it, you didn't bring canned soup."

"Luc—that's the chef from La Mer—offered to make it. You think I should have said no?"

"You're a terrible liar, Mark. Why would Luc do that?" She sat down. "Look, you and I both know where you want to take this. But it'd be nice if you'd just step back and let her be. She's not in the best place emotionally."

Her warning set his teeth on edge. It seemed like nobody wanted him and Hilary to be together. "Are you saying I had something to do with that?"

Josephine studied her impeccable manicure and frowned as though she'd found a flaw, which was doubtful. The kind of places women like her went to didn't screw up. She looked up at him, grimacing like she'd just bitten into a clam and gotten sand. "No."

"Then what is it?"

"Bebe's back."

"Her cousin, right?"

"That's one word for her. And whenever she's around, things aren't good for Hilary. Bebe is just bad news, start to finish."

"I'm sensing that you don't like her."

"She's a worthless skank. She's doing every-thing in her power to live just like her mother, and it bothers her that Hilary won't. That she's trying for something better."

"Yeah, Bebe told me about the whole ménage thing."

"Oh god, she did?" Josephine folded her arms in front of her and looked to the side, her teeth on edge. "Unbelievable. It's like she thinks it's some kind of badge of honor to have lived through that childhood."

"Well…isn't it?"

Her jaw slackened. "Are you serious?"

"To survive something like that?" Mark wasn't sure if he would've been able to. "It didn't sound pretty at all."

"Surviving is what any animal would do. It's making something of yourself that earns the badge. Nobody can choose how they were born and raised, but everyone can choose how they're going to live."

Her words robbed him of air, and he swallowed a small gasp as his heart pounded with something that felt awfully like a bitter old hope. "What if they can't?" he said hoarsely.

Her flat gaze locked with his. "Then they'll end up like their parents—or worse."

MARK DROVE BACK TO LA MER. HE'D FORGOTTEN about the dinner he had scheduled with Gavin and his wife Amandine until Larry the Maître d' had called. As he sped down the road, Mark couldn't stop thinking about what Josephine had said. *They'll end up like their parents—or worse.*

Was he somehow becoming like his father, going after one woman after another in a string of seemingly carefree relationships that were actually killing him little by little?

Everyone thought Salazar had the greatest life. He'd been born handsome, charming and wealthy, he'd married one of the most beautiful women of his generation, and—best of all—his wife didn't seem to care about his mistresses.

And yet, hadn't he lost something in all that?

Mark thought about how his mother had changed. When he was young she had laughed every day, spent a lot of time with the family... She'd arranged for fun vacations and other family gatherings.

But now...

The Fourth of the July party was a huge aberration. The most the family ever managed was the annual Christmas party, if either of his parents felt like delegating the task to one of their assistants. The oldest of the children, Dane, didn't even pretend to want to come. He generally found a reason not to be available—usually work. Apparently even though the western world didn't work on Christmas, Asia did, so he'd spend his Christmas there doing one of his deals.

But that wasn't all. Mark knew his father had been forced to let go of the one great love of his life because he couldn't change his ways. And it wasn't just the woman he'd missed. He'd fathered a son with her, but hadn't been aware of that fact until recently because he hadn't been able to do what he needed to do to keep her. So he'd missed that son's entire childhood.

That didn't feel like a great life.

At La Mer, Gavin and his wife Amandine were already seated. The lovebirds sat closely, chatting in low voices. Amandine laughed softly at something Gavin said and touched the tip of his nose with hers. The sight made Mark happy—he was glad they'd been able to work out their marital issues. But a small pang of envy twisted in his heart at the same time. He wanted it too—this kind of bliss and openness. The problem was he didn't know how to get it, and it shamed him that he felt something as ugly as envy for his friend and his wife.

"Hey," Mark said. "Sorry I'm late."

Amandine straightened up. "No problem. We just got here ourselves. You look good, Mark." She gave him a friendly smile. She was one of the sweetest women he knew, and even if he'd been an hour late, she still would've said, "We just got here."

"Where have you been? Larry said you were gone more or less all afternoon."

"Oh. I stopped by your firm earlier, but Sally said you were in a meeting. Then I went to Josephine's place to see if Hilary needed anything."

"And that took you all afternoon?" Gavin raised an eyebrow. "I'm pretty sure she doesn't have a long list of things she needs."

Mark knew the comment was intended as a jibe, but it still annoyed him. What did his best friend know about what Hilary needed? She was the one who catered to him all the time, not the other way around. "You're just real sure, huh? Have you called or checked up on Hilary at all?"

"Well, no, but I'm sure—"

"You know what? She did tell me what she wanted," Mark said. "And you're right, it wasn't a long list, but at the top was an assistant who could help her."

"Really?" Gavin said, and Amandine's face fell.

"Oh shoot," she said. "It's all my fault. I should've known."

"It's got nothing to do with you, love," Gavin said, but she shook her head.

"No, it does. I hate having an assistant around, so I've sort of gone without since Brooke quit. But I'm sure that just means Hilary now has more on her plate."

"She hasn't complained about it being too much for her."

"You can be *so* obtuse. Just because she doesn't complain doesn't mean you can make her do a two-person job by herself. She's not a robot."

A frown creased Gavin's forehead. "You're right. I should've thought about that."

"I'll hire an assistant ASAP," Amandine promised. "I'm glad you brought it up, Mark. I'm sure Hilary wouldn't have. She seems to thrive on mountains of work, but that doesn't mean it's good for her."

Amandine was wrong. Hilary didn't thrive when her to-do list was bursting with tasks. She just worked even harder so that she wouldn't disappoint her boss.

Then it hit Mark. She was trying to be everything to Gavin, so he'd never fire her, no matter what. But why would she do that? She could probably do better—the same money for better hours and less stress—by going elsewhere.

"So what's going on between the two of you?" Gavin sipped his white. "You sent her flowers and chocolates every day, went to the charity event together...then you suddenly stopped, and now you were at her place for hours. What gives?"

"We're dating."

"Seriously?"

"You think I do those things with just any woman?"

"Well…yeah." Mark gave him a sour look, and Gavin spread his hands. "Hey, what can I say? But honestly, Hilary? She's not your type, and you don't do relationships."

Mark ground his teeth. At the rate things were going, he was going to be down to his gums soon. "She totally *is* my type, and I *do* do relationships."

"Three months here and there doesn't count. Besides, if anything goes wrong during the next quarter, you're on your own. I'm not taking sides on this one."

"Thanks for the vote of confidence, buddy," Mark snapped. "My own fuc"—he bit the word off in deference to Amandine—"best friend thinks I'm going to fail."

Gavin's eyebrows rose, his eyes round and unblinking. "Totally wrong. I think you're going to lose interest."

Mark was about to fire off another sharp retort when Amandine smiled and laid a hand on Gavin's arm. "Please excuse him. Of course you can do relationships. You just haven't met the right woman yet. Your time will come. Or maybe it already has with Hilary."

Her soothing voice and words deflated Mark's irritation. Technically it wasn't fair for him to be angry at Gavin. He was right not to take sides in the situation. He'd often said Hilary was worth her weight in gold, and he wouldn't want to lose her if Mark fumbled the ball.

But it hurt and annoyed him that people expected him to screw up.

FIFTEEN

HILARY WANTED TO RETURN TO THE OFFICE on Monday, but Gavin had texted her to take both Monday and Tuesday off. After four full days of rest she felt fine. Not surprising—she'd never taken so much time off to do nothing except sleep and then sleep some more. Then there was the pampering. Jo had been too busy, but Mark was coming by every day and spending hours with her, heating up whatever his chef had decided to make for them and watching movies. They'd started out with horror flicks—his choice, not hers. When she'd laughed at the scary scenes instead of jumping into his arms, he stopped the movie and said, "Okay, never mind. What are you in the mood for?"

She didn't have to think. "*The Sound of Music!* It's my favorite."

He flung an arm over his eyes. "Agh! You're killing me. I can't stand that movie."

"Really? Why?"

"Don't you know? Men hate musicals."

"That's not true."

"Okay, all hetero men. But, okay. Your wish is my command."

As they watched, Mark even sang a few of the songs with her. For a man who claimed to hate musicals, he had a decent voice. Then they sat through *Mary Poppins*. Finally he brought out the Julie Andrews version of *Cinderella*, which Hilary hadn't seen yet.

"We can watch something else," she suggested, feeling guilty. She would've been pretty annoyed if she'd had to endure hours of zombie movies. "Maybe something with lots of mindless violence and car chases?"

"Nope. We're watching *Cinderella*. It's your sick day," he'd said with a small grin, hitting play.

She rested her head in the crook of his neck and watched the musical, feeling like she was Cinderella. She couldn't remember the last time somebody had shown this much hands-on interest in her wellbeing. She was supposed to be able to stand on her own and take care of herself.

HILARY PULLED HER HAIR BACK INTO A TIGHT BUN and put on her usual conservative work clothes. Her complexion was still on the pale side, but it was nothing a little makeup couldn't fix.

The doorbell rang, and Mark came in. "I told you to lock the door," he called out.

"Josephine just left, and I'm about to head out as well," she said.

"Where?" he said, poking his head into her room. "Are you going to work?"

"Yes."

"It's the third of July."

"So?"

"Nobody's going to be there."

She rolled her eyes. "Are you sure you and Gavin are best friends?"

"We're close enough, and I know things you'd never guess." He scowled. "And I know you even better. You're going in even though you aren't feeling a hundred percent."

"I took four days off, Mark. That was more than enough time to recuperate."

"I don't think so. I think you need to take the rest of the week off."

"The rest of the week?!"

"Yeah. It's already Wednesday. Tomorrow's the fourth, and nobody's working on Friday."

"That's ridiculous. Everyone at owm is going to work…well…except maybe the janitors."

"And most of the admins," Mark added.

"But I need to go in. Gavin will be there."

"You know Gavin's taking four days off, right?"

She gaped at him. "He is?" Then she remembered. He had actually mentioned something about that a few months back.

"His family's coming for the Fourth of July party at his place, and he's gotta play host," Mark said. "And you don't have to do anything for Amandine either. She's looking for a new assistant and already has a temp, She'll probably get somebody permanent soon."

Hilary filed that information away. She knew why Amandine had a hard time hiring people. The woman didn't want somebody hovering over her all the time. Her best friend had filled the slot for a while, and that had been okay, but now she was gone to pursue a new career.

But Kim would be a good fit. She was the right age and excellent at her job. She'd know how to make Amandine feel comfortable.

"So as you can plainly see," Mark continued, "taking the rest of the week off is the most logical thing to do."

"But—"

"No *buts*. Just a yes will be fine." Mark brushed the back of his index finger along her cheek. The contact made her face tingle with heat. "I'm worried about you, that's all."

Hilary's insides melted at the simple declaration.

When people wanted her to take time off, it was generally so they could benefit from it. Bebe had often wanted her to skip school so they could hang out with boys or go smoke pot in some empty lot. Her mother and aunt and Tim had asked when they wanted her to run errands—do the grocery shopping or have the power turned back on because they'd forgotten to pay the bill and were too tired and hung over to talk to the utility company. Until Mark, nobody had insisted she played hookey just to take care of herself. "You know, I don't know if I like this you."

"What about it?"

"You're bossy."

He laughed. "Me? Bossy? Never. If I were bossy, we wouldn't be having this conversation. And you wouldn't have been telling me to go home because I'd get whatever you have."

"Oh really? What would have happened instead?"

A wicked gleam entered his eyes. "For one, we would've C & R'd." He put his arms around her and pulled her down on her bed. She landed with a gasp, then laughed.

"Okay. I can deal with that. And then what?"

"Then I'd've kissed you back to health."

She looked up at him. "What is this? Some kind of fairytale?"

"Yup. It's called Ailing Beauty. It's kind of obscure, though…not too many people know about it. It took me a long time to discover it myself."

"Care to share this incredibly obscure tale?"

"Well… Once upon a time, there was a beautiful, sexy and terribly overworked princess."

She swallowed a giggle.

"Her bossy king made her work so much that one day she fainted despite her best efforts not to. Instead of nursing her back to health, the king sent her to her room to recover on her own."

"Wow. What a terrible king," she joked.

"I know. Anyway, don't interrupt. You're going to miss the good part."

"All right. Go on."

"A humble and handsome prince passing by saw this untenable situation and volunteered to watch over her. Many people protested, including the princess. Nursing was a woman's job, they said. But the prince wasn't going to allow some ridiculous stereotype to get in the way. He knew this princess needed him even if she didn't know it herself."

"Of course." Was she getting breathless? She'd asked him to tell her to humor him, but this was sweeter than expected. Butterflies in her stomach fluttered at the close proximity of his body—his warmth and masculine scent. She put a hand over his hard, muscular chest. Their hearts seemed to beat in unison.

"So every day he went to the castle kitchen and ordered the chef to make the most delicious and nutritious food in the entire kingdom. That was the only thing worthy of passing her beautiful lips."

Her mouth twitched in a beginning of a smile, and the shell around her heart cracked.

"Then he made sure the princess ate every bite of the specially prepared food, so she could recover her strength."

"Ah."

"The princess found the prince to be kind, and the prince thought the princess was the most wonderful woman he'd ever seen, but then he started to worry. What if the king needed her before she was fully recovered? Then all the prince's efforts would be for naught."

"What a terrible waste." She giggled.

"Precisely." He tapped the tip of her nose. "So a few days later, when the princess got dressed to go back to her royal duties, the prince stopped her and demanded proof of her good health."

When he didn't continue, she said, "So what did she do?"

"She didn't do anything." His eyes bore into hers. He was so close, his breath fanned against her lips. They tingled in anticipation. "It was the prince who finally said, 'I know what to do.'"

"So what did he do?" she whispered, her gaze drifting down to his lips.

"This." Mark's mouth closed over hers, and she trembled. There was something so intimate about his kiss, like he could read her completely through that single connection. She pulled him closer for a better taste. It was all Mark and sugar-sweet promises.

A week ago, what they were doing would have scared her to death. She didn't want to believe in empty gestures. But now…she wasn't so sure they were empty. Everything Mark had done was too much work for a short-term, meaningless fling. Even if everything between them were to end tomorrow, she wanted to reach out and grab him now with no regrets.

He slid his big, hot hand along her leg. It slipped under her skirt, and she loved the slow pulsing it created inside her. New and pleasurable feelings coursed through her. No man had ever brought out this sharp and addictive chemistry.

He nuzzled her jaw line and neck, taking his time, then very carefully ran his hand along the under curve of her breasts. She felt the touch as if she wasn't wearing anything. And she couldn't help but imagine how much nicer it would be if she were fully naked, and he was touching her skin-to-skin.

"So damn soft," he breathed. "Hilary."

"Yes?"

"Will you make love with me? I'm dying to take this to the next level, but if you aren't sure…"

This was her final chance to turn him away and protect herself. But if she pulled back now, it'd signal the end to all this. They'd go to his family party together, and that would be it. No man would want to be around a woman who pulled back over and over again without risking even a fraction of herself.

She cupped his face between her hands. "I'm very sure."

He closed his eyes and whispered, "Thank god."

Suddenly his relief and joy broke a tight vise around her heart. With a wicked grin, she pushed him back and straddled him. Her skirt bunched up around her hips, but she didn't care.

"You drive me crazy, you know," she murmured. "You aren't supposed to be this persistent or intriguing or sexy."

He grinned up at her. "I am irresistible, aren't I?"

"And so modest." She explored his body with her hands. He was all sinew and thick, strong muscles underneath the carefully fitted clothes. He held still as she unbuttoned the crisp white shirt and spread her hands over the expanse of his powerful chest. Dark hair dusted the smooth skin, and she rolled his small nipples with her fingers, then tugged on them.

He sucked in a breath. "Damn."

"Damn good or damn bad?"

"Damn good and do it again."

With a soft hum of satisfaction, she moved her hands down the ridges of his stomach and put her mouth where her fingers had been. He was surprisingly sensitive to her touch. She liked that. It made her feel powerful and strong, like she could do anything she wished and keep him in her power.

She stripped him and studied his gorgeous body with appreciation. Maybe the famous Pryce profile wasn't limited to just faces. There was absolutely nothing wrong with his physique. If somebody made a sculpture of his nude body, she could buy it and put that in the office and call it art. It was that perfect, and this perfection was all hers.

His cock got even harder under her scrutiny. It was long and thick and she couldn't help but send him a long wicked glance. If he knew what she was fantasizing about…

"Yes?" he said as though he read her mind.

Out of the three things that had flashed through her mind, she chose the one that enticed her the most. She ran her nails along his inner thighs, and his ribcage jerked as his breathing grew rougher and more uneven. She looked up at him with big doe eyes, licked her lips, and said, "Watch."

MARK THOUGHT HE'D DIE RIGHT THERE WHEN SHE pulled the head of his cock into her mouth. Holding eye contact, she hollowed her cheeks and sucked on him. Damn… His muscles tightened as pleasure built. He'd had other women go down on him, but Hilary somehow made him feel like he'd shoot right then and there. The fact that this was Hilary's mouth on him, and Hilary's eyes on his, pushed him until he was teetering on the edge.

But that wouldn't do. He hadn't pursued her so he would embarrass himself like some inexperienced high school kid. Instinctively he knew getting this far was just the first step. There were still obstacles to overcome if he wanted Hilary to be with him beyond this moment.

He pulled out with a soft pop. She looked at him quizzically. Without answering the unspoken question in her gaze, he brought her up and kissed her openly.

She responded enthusiastically and sucked on his tongue. His balls tightened. Shit. His baser self wanted to go back to what they'd been doing before, but he didn't. He wanted to hear her scream his name when she came.

He unbuttoned and tugged at her clothes until she was naked except for the matching lacy bra and panties. They were cut conservatively, making her look like an innocent angel about to be seduced. He kissed her breast, then pulled the nipple into his mouth right through the fabric. Her back arched, and she wrapped her legs around his hips. His cock settled into the folds, and he groaned at how wet she was.

"Baby, you're so hot," he said.

She laughed, the sound breathless. "You make me hot."

He rocked against her, and she moaned, the deep and throaty sound going to his head like the best whiskey money could buy. He pulled her panties off. She looked so wantonly innocent with her legs spread and her modest bra covering her breasts. She was so perfect it hurt.

But now it was his turn. "Watch."

A long slow lick along the folds of her sex yielded a honeyed taste. She was so slick and hot, he thought he could come just from going down on her. Her thighs quivered, and he loved it that he was giving her this pleasure. But he wanted to give her more. The need to prove he could make her happy in bed drove him, and he wasn't going to stop now that he had the chance.

He pulled her clit into his mouth and used his tongue on it. A tortured moan tore from her throat, and her hand clenched the sheet. Her breath hitched as if she hadn't done this in a while…she hadn't had anything this hot in a long time. Maybe all her previous lovers had sucked in bed. Maybe they'd been impotent.

He sensed her control slipping, and then she shattered, back bowed and knuckles white. She pressed a fist against her mouth to muffle her scream, but he pushed it away.

"Let me hear your pleasure, Hilary," he said. "I want to hear it."

She sobbed, tears streaking from the corners of her eyes. He kissed them away, exultant he'd been able to take her to this high of a climax. She shuddered for a while. When it had eased into minor tremors, she whispered, "That was amazing."

He grinned. "I'm a pretty amazing guy," he said shamelessly, absurdly happy with the world. "You're gorgeous when you come."

She flushed. "Now you're embarrassing me."

He barked out a laugh. "Are you kidding me? You let me devour you like that, and now you're embarrassed?"

"Oh hush." She reached downward and took him in her hand. "You're still really hard."

"I wanted to wait until we could do it again. I want to come with you."

HILARY RUBBED HER THUMB OVER THE TIP OF HIS erection, spreading his slickness all over the head. "So do I, Mark."

She couldn't think of anything better than coming apart in his arms with him following her into sweet oblivion. Reaching behind her, she undid the bra clasp and dropped it on the floor. Now they were both fully naked with nothing between them.

"Do you have a condom?" she asked.

He made a show of thinking hard. "Hmm… There might *possibly* be one in…my right front pants pocket."

"Prepared, aren't you?"

"Hopeful. I've wanted to be with you like this for a long time."

She smiled and retrieved the protection from his trousers. She sheathed him and murmured, "I want to be in control of this."

"Whatever feels right. I want you to be comfortable."

She let out a throaty laugh. The last thing she was was comfortable. She was so needy it wasn't even funny.

She ran her fingernails along his balls and heard his breath catch. His cock twitched at her every teasing touch. She loved that. She couldn't believe she had this powerful, gorgeous man at her disposal…to do with as she wished for their mutual satisfaction.

She straddled him and fed his cock into her, slow inch by slow inch. He felt enormous, the delicious stretching of her inner muscles almost too much to bear. She couldn't remember the last time she was this wet and eager. But most importantly, she felt safe.

Mark would never hurt her.

He groaned when she was fully seated. She linked her hands with his and bit her lower lip. Slowly she started moving. He matched her rhythm, but he didn't rush her. He hadn't been kidding when he'd said he wanted her to be comfortable. Slowly she picked up the tempo, as her body craved more of the sweet friction between them. Her fingers tightened, and her toes curled as he placed his feet flat on the bed and pumped into her. It seemed to push him even deeper and harder into her body, and she sighed as her blood sizzled in the beginning of an orgasm.

"Say my name, baby," he said, his voice rough. "Say it."

She screamed his name and came. He made one final hard push and joined her. His teeth were clenched tight, and the muscles of his neck stood out starkly. His hands tightened, but he made sure he didn't crush hers. His dark gaze focused on her, and she knew he loved this passionate side of her.

Breathing hard, she collapsed on him. His heart thundered under her ear, and she closed her eyes to savor the moment. This was beyond lovely and nothing like she'd experienced before. She'd always thought being with him like this would shackle her and strip her of whatever control she needed to be strong. Paradoxically enough, she felt more liberated than ever before in his arms. It was like he'd freed her from her long-held belief about dating acceptable men who didn't excite her. There was power in being able to respond to her man fully and honestly and wantonly.

But…

She was never lucky in love. None of the Rosenberg women were.

She clung to him, willing this to be an exception. Anything else would ruin her.

SIXTEEN

EARLY THE NEXT MORNING, MARK WATCHED Hilary sleep in his bed. She hadn't been comfortable staying at Jo's if he was going to stick around, and he had no intention of spending the night alone, not when he finally had Hilary where he wanted her—in bed with him.

They'd been busy breaking in his hardly touched kitchen, the well-used bar, the living room, the dining room, the bathroom and of course the bedroom. Hilary had been insatiable, and he loved the passionate side of her that fed his own need. She was the most perfect lover a man could ask for. And it was great that she wasn't self-conscious about her curvy body. He adored her hourglass shape—it was full of sexy feminine curves and dips that begged to be explored.

Right now he was hard again, and his baser instincts said he should wake her up, but he slipped out of the bed instead. She should get *some* sleep. He didn't want her to relapse. It still bugged him she wouldn't see a doctor. What if she had something more serious than just being overworked?

So he went out and got various bagels and cream cheese. *Not so good at cooking, but great at buying*, he thought to himself. And just in case she wanted some variety, he also tossed in a couple of croissants. He didn't know a single woman who didn't love croissants, even if they generally avoided "evil" carbs.

Hilary didn't care, and that was another thing he loved about her. A woman who enjoyed her food was super hot.

When he returned, he found her in the kitchen, dressed in his robe, her hair mussed. Sharp desire and need dug into his chest, stealing his breath away, but he pushed them aside for the moment, searching for any signs of fatigue in her. He felt a small pang of guilt…but it was pretty small.

She smiled at him and yawned. "I made some coffee," she said. "Hope you don't mind."

"Mi casa es tu casa." He plopped the paper bag full of baked goodies on the table. "See if there's anything you like. I'll get some plates."

"I'm sure whatever you have in the bag is great." She typed something on her phone.

"You texting Josephine to let her know what an amazing night you had?" he asked from the kitchen.

"No! I'm sending a note to Amandine. I know the perfect person to be her new assistant."

He selected two bone-china plates and some pieces from the heirloom Nathan and Hayes silverware set his mother had given him. He'd never had a chance to use either, but now seemed like a good time. "You do?"

"Yes. We professional assistants network, you know." She finished her text and put the phone down.

He finished setting the table, complete with the fresh coffee she'd made. "You should've done that months ago instead of taking on more work. It's not like Gavin's too poor to hire someone for his wife."

"I didn't think it was that big of a deal." Hilary sat and picked up a croissant. "Amandine doesn't like having personal assistants. She seems to think they're too CIA-like or something, always watching her and stuff."

"That's crazy."

"Just the way she is. She didn't grow up with money the way you did."

He stopped in the middle of spreading cream cheese on his bagel. He couldn't identify it, but there was an odd undertone in the way she'd said "the way you did." "Does it bother you?"

"What?" she said, buttering her croissant.

"About my upbringing."

"Not really. I just know we grew up very differently." She frowned at the heavy silver knife in her hand. "Does it bother you that I'm not like your other girlfriends?"

"Good god, no. I'm glad you're different. If you were anything like the others, I'd be bored to tears by now." He'd been watching and speculating about Hilary long before he'd approached her. He wanted to see if the reality would match his imagination. So far, it had surpassed it.

"The party's today right?" she asked.

"Yeah. It's at the grove."

"How many people are coming?"

"Basically everyone, except maybe for Blaine and his fiancée." Blaine was Salazar's illegitimate son.

"Ceinlys didn't invite him?"

"No, he got an invitation. But he might avoid the whole shindig because it's awkward." Also he didn't like Ceinlys. Mark had noticed that, and in some ways he couldn't blame the guy. He probably thought—incorrectly—that if Ceinlys hadn't been in the picture Salazar might have married his mother. From what Mark had gathered, Blaine grew up dirt poor. Mark wondered how he would've reacted if the situation had been reversed.

"Okay, well, I need to go to Josephine's place to pick out something to wear," she said. "Afterward, I'll meet you back here."

"You don't have to do that. I already have your clothes here."

"You do?"

"Yeah. I asked Josephine to choose a good outfit for you."

She fidgeted. "I don't want you to make me look like I'm something that I'm not."

"Which is what?"

"Knowing Josephine, she probably bought the most expensive stuff possible, which means it's going to be something I could never afford on my salary. That's not how I envisioned this…outing."

"Hilary, don't worry about money. I want you to wear something that'll be comfortable for you. But some of my distant cousins and aunts are snobbish, and it would be unpleasant to give them something to talk about." Then there was his mother, who hadn't said anything directly to him yet about his dating Hilary, although she had to be unhappy about it. She'd made it clear she didn't approve of his choice.

"I don't know."

"Just humor me, okay? Besides, think of the time we can save. We can use that for something better than arguing about your outfit."

"Which is…?"

He gave her a wicked grin. "Let me show you."

HILARY WAS FORCED TO ADMIT MARK HAD DONE well to have Jo select her outfit. It was a comfortable coral orange sundress with spaghetti straps and cute casual shoes that were comfortable without looking too under-dressy. Jo had even included a wide-brimmed hat and sunglasses that went well with the outfit. The hat turned out to be a huge bonus; the sky was cloudless and the day scorching. The grove had plenty of shade, but it was always nice to have extra protection to prevent burning. And being a redhead, Hilary was particularly sensitive to the sun.

Mark took her to the center of the action where his parents were. Salazar and Ceinlys Pryce stood next to each other and greeted every member of the family who arrived. He was handsome—an older version of Mark. He'd shed his usual suit for the picnic and donned pale shorts and a sapphire blue polo shirt that brought out his eyes. Ceinlys hadn't dressed down quite as much as her husband. In a pristine white dress and a matching hat with netting, she looked like European royalty. Unlike Gavin and his wife at Eliza's charity event, Salazar and Ceinlys seemed to take great care to avoid any sort of contact with each other. It couldn't be easy to stand close enough to appear as a couple, but still avoid touching each other, even accidentally.

The weird thing was, nobody seemed to notice it…but maybe this was just a normal thing at Pryce family gatherings. Salazar patted Mark on the shoulder, and Ceinlys gave him an air kiss.

"Mom, Dad, you know Hilary," Mark said.

Salazar's face split into a smile. "Welcome. I hope you enjoy the picnic."

"Thank you, sir."

"Call me Salazar," he said. "Sir makes me sound so old."

Ceinlys's gaze flicked to Mark's arm around Hilary's waist then rose back to Hilary's face. There was something that felt like repugnance in the way Ceinlys looked at her. Hilary stole a quick glance at Mark, but he seemed oblivious from the way he was grinning at his mother.

Then Ceinlys's eyes changed, becoming suddenly warm and inviting, and she smiled at Hilary. "Welcome, my dear. How lovely to see you again."

"Thank you," Hilary managed. She was sure she hadn't imagined the earlier distaste, but she wouldn't make a big deal about it either. This was Mark's family, and they were important to him. She didn't want to ruin the day by being critical.

"Where's Shane?" Mark asked.

"He missed his flight." Irritation put a little line between his mother's eyebrows. "I offered to send him the family jet, but he said no. I should've done it anyway."

The arrival of some cousins cut their conversation short. There were so many more people than Hilary had expected. She recognized most of the immediate family—except for Dane. She wasn't sure if he'd come. Dane was a bit of a recluse when it came to his family gatherings from what she'd heard. She'd done some digging to see what kind of boss Kim might end up with if she managed to stay with the Pryce family business, and nothing about Dane indicated he would be easy to work for. Thank god Amandine was serious about hiring somebody. It wasn't like being an executive administrative assistant, but Kim could still make good money and build a great network. Amandine and Gavin traveled in the very top social circles. Getting introduced to those people couldn't hurt, and when you knew them, unexpected opportunities just seemed to crop up. Hilary had contacted Amandine that morning to make doubly sure Kim would have the best chance at the job.

"Smile," Mark said, squeezing her hand. "You look tense."

"I'm not," Hilary said. "I'm just wondering which one Dane is."

"Don't." He gave her a lopsided grin. "You don't want to meet that ogre."

She swallowed a startled laugh. "What?"

"He's not the most pleasant guy to be around. Sort of a party pooper. I'm not even sure he's here. He usually doesn't bother."

He introduced her to tons of cousins and other far-flung relatives. She was good with faces and names, but it eventually became overwhelming.

Everyone was so nice and sweet, doing their best to make her feel welcome. She couldn't help but compare his family to hers. If she'd brought Mark to Lila's home for a Fourth of July barbecue, it would've been a disaster with Bebe plastering herself all over him and Lila going on about her "great love affair" with Tim. None of them would know how to be gracious, and even if they tried to make Mark feel comfortable, they'd only end up alienating him.

Despite their sweet lovemaking earlier that day, Hilary suddenly felt like there was a chasm between her and Mark that nothing could bridge. She couldn't imagine how all these people would react if they knew the truth about her background. They'd probably gasp…or flee in horror.

And would Mark stand by her?

She shook herself inwardly. *Stop getting ahead of yourself.* They'd only been together for about a month. She was expecting too much.

Some time later, a few cousins came by to challenge Mark to some blind testing. Apparently guessing the wine vintage and its year correctly was his party trick, and they were certain they'd found a few that Mark wouldn't be able to pinpoint.

"Wanna come with?" one of the cousins asked Hilary. "You can watch him embarrass himself."

Mark gave him a pitying look. "You mean like the last time? When I embarrassed myself so much I relieved you of five hundred bucks on that side bet?" He turned to Hilary and said, "There's nothing I don't know about wine." It was in a low voice…but still loud enough for everyone else to hear.

"I need to go to the restroom first," she said. "Why don't I meet you guys at the bar?"

"Perfect!" the cousin said and the group dragged Mark away.

Hilary reflected as she washed up in the restroom. It was illuminating to see the people Mark had grown up with. They were so different from her family. Elegant, well-educated and cultured, they spoke smoothly and laughed often. It wasn't just the money that made them the way they were either. It was something as innate as their DNA, something Hilary and her family just did not have. She stared at herself in the mirror over the sink. If she'd spent more time with them, would she learn to be like them too? Or at least be good at faking it?

She dried her hands with paper towels and made her way to the bar. The family had set it up near the picnic area.

"Enjoying the party, dear?"

She turned at Ceinlys's soft voice. "Yes, ma'am."

Ceinlys's mouth smiled. "That's good to hear. I hate it when guests don't enjoy themselves."

"Well, this is quite a party."

"Thank you." She gestured toward a path running into the orange trees. "Hilary, do you mind if we chat briefly? Something's been weighing heavily on my mind, and I want to know how to resolve the matter."

"I don't know how I can be of help, but sure."

They walked into the rows of trees, their green leaves glossy with vitality. Bees and butterflies flew about, and Hilary suddenly realized that Ceinlys's hat had netting for reasons other than fashion.

"I'm pretty sure you've seen that YouTube video by now," Ceinlys began.

"Actually, I haven't." Hilary didn't have the stomach to relive the humiliating moment. "But I can imagine how it looks."

"That's remarkable. Most wouldn't have been able to resist."

"I was there."

"True," Ceinlys admitted. "I find the whole situation rather convenient. Or inconvenient, depending on one's point of view." She paused and pursed her mouth. "I had to wonder who would record it and put it up on YouTube. And to what purpose? For the longest time I thought it had to be somebody in our social circle, or perhaps one of those horrid gossip-mongers who like to believe they're legitimate journalists. A blogger." She nearly sneered the last word. "They're always looking for publicity and validation by having their so-called work go viral."

"I'm sorry I got Mark mixed up in all this," Hilary said, pretty certain that what Ceinlys wanted was an apology.

"That's an interesting sentiment…your being sorry." Ceinlys gazed at a small green orange hanging from a branch on eye level. "I tracked the woman down."

"Who?"

"Your ex-boyfriend's fiancée."

Hilary tilted her head. Ceinlys was still studying the orange. Had she thought the fiancée would give her some dirt about Hilary and Walt?

Ceinlys was a bit of a gossip herself. She took photos and posted them on Facebook, although she was pretty discreet from what Hilary had heard. Hilary wasn't good enough to be included in Ceinlys's circle, of course, and she wondered if Ceinlys wanted to share some angry comments from the fiancée with all her friends on Facebook.

"It wasn't easy to find her," Ceinlys said. "My men looked for her at law firms in the area. Then they tried hospitals, that being the next logical place. Unfortunately, she didn't exist."

The Pryce family undoubtedly had their own investigators who could handle sensitive matters discreetly. Hilary knew that Gavin's family had a big firm on retainer. But she couldn't understand why Ceinlys wanted to find the fiancée so badly.

"They finally found her at an acting school," Ceinlys continued. "She's an actress, did you know that? Such a cliché, isn't it?"

"I…guess. But what does that have to do with the video?"

"She was playing the role of your boyfriend's fiancée."

"What?" Hilary found the words hard to process, like English had suddenly become a foreign language to her. "Why would anyone do something like that?"

"She said a woman approached her…and paid her to take the role."

Hilary sucked in a breath. Despite the heat, ice seemed to form in her heart and spread across her chest. "But…why would—?"

"She claimed she didn't realize the…encounter was being filmed, which I know is a lie. At least she didn't insult my intelligence further. She admitted she found it 'great exposure.'" Ceinlys finally yanked on the orange and tossed it on the ground. It rolled toward Hilary. "She seems to believe that it will further her career. At my son's expense."

What about her? Hilary was the one who'd thought her boyfriend cheated on her, that she'd been going down the path of her mother and aunt. But according to what Ceinlys had just said, that wasn't the case. Hilary placed a hand on her suddenly stiff neck and gazed up at the canopy of leaves above her. This…this had to be some kind of joke.

"Then I wondered: who would go to the trouble of creating such a scene, much less film it and post it on YouTube? The ip address of the uploader is located in L.A. It's a café near your address. The Orangery Café." Ceinlys watched Hilary the way a hungry owl would a mouse. "Does that ring a bell?"

God. That was the café she often stopped by to surf the net or have some "me" time away from her aunt on weekends and holidays. It had free wifi and comfortable chairs.

"Take the video down, my dear. And never come near my family again."

"Wait a minute. You think *I* put—?"

Ceinlys reached into her purse and pulled out a small brown envelope. They were deep enough into the grove that the sounds of revelry were far behind them. "Take this."

Hilary kept her hands at her sides. "What is it?"

"Money, of course. That's what you want, isn't it? So take it and go away."

"Ceinlys, I had nothing to do with that video." She couldn't believe what the older woman was accusing her of. Her stomach roiled at the unfairness of it all. "I haven't even been to that café in the past month, what with all the projects I have."

"Among which would be the project of dating my son?" Ceinlys shook her head. "I appreciate a woman with ambition, but I also prefer that she be aware of her limits. I know everything about you. I can ruin you and make Gavin fire you."

"Gavin won't fire me." Of that Hilary was sure. She'd made herself absolutely indispensable to her boss.

"Oh, I think he will. I shall make certain of it." Ceinlys finally cracked a small, genuine smile. "You see, I know you lied on your job application."

Cold sweat trickled down Hilary's back, and her hands felt clammy. There was a nasty sour tang in her mouth. "What are you talking about?" she managed through nerveless lips.

"The application asked if you've ever done drugs, didn't it? And your response was 'no.'"

Hilary's heart pounded, and she felt like blood was shooting upward, all the way to the top of her skull from the way it roared in her head.

"Unless things have changed recently, I'm sure ecstasy counts. When Gavin finds out, he'll have to fire you. He's let more than a few workers go already for lying on their job applications, and it would send the wrong message to be seen playing favorites." Ceinlys's eyes swept Hilary up and down. "You aren't that special. And those workers who lost their jobs would be more than happy to sue for discrimination and wrongful termination if he kept you."

Ceinlys was right. And Gavin would fire her rather than deal with multi-million dollar lawsuits from angry former employees. Everything Hilary had worked for would be lost, and she doubted anybody would hire her afterward. The story of her lying on the job application would get out, and Ceinlys would make sure she'd never find a decent paying position in the state.

"I'm not doing this to hurt you," Ceinlys said softly. "I simply want you out of the picture. Whatever your end game may be, Hilary, I won't see my son used by people like you and your cousin."

"My cousin?" Hilary clutched her clammy hands together to stop them from shaking. "What did she do?"

"That's a very good question. She went to his restaurant early Friday afternoon…and stayed there for quite some time."

Ceinlys was lying. She had to be. "How do you know?"

"I watched her from my car." Ceinlys pulled out a photo showing a woman dressed in cut-offs walking into La Mer. It was taken from behind the woman, but Hilary instantly knew it was Bebe. "I considered going in, but thought I'd just let things develop. I understand from the maître d' that she was in Mark's private office the entire time."

Hilary's hands dropped to her sides, and she stared at Ceinlys. The breakfast croissants sat in Hilary's belly in an indigestible lump of bitterness.

Mark had never mentioned he'd seen Bebe one-on-one.

Then she remembered how Mark had shown up at Jo's place all of a sudden after ignoring her for days…on Friday. Why the change of heart? What had her cousin offered?

"My men were very thorough. I know everything about you and your cousin. As far as I can tell, Mark's never done a ménage a trois. Perhaps you and your cousin thought you could get him to share a bed with the two of you, just as your mothers shared a man. You should reconsider. Two quarterlies don't add up to a forever."

Shaking, Hilary put a hand over her mouth. She was cold, then hot, and she couldn't stop trembling. The breeze seemed woefully inadequate to cool her, and sweat popped along her hairline. She blinked a few times to clear her vision.

"If you're going to be sick, the bathroom's over there." Ceinlys gestured to Hilary's left. "You seem like a survivor. I'm sure you'll make a wise decision."

Without taking the envelope Ceinlys had offered, Hilary stumbled away, as fast as her clumsy feet could carry her, away from this horrible woman, away from the Pryce family…and away from Mark.

SEVENTEEN

ILARY RAN TO THE PARKING LOT. SHE HAD to get out of there before she got sick. A part of her wondered if she should confront Mark, but she couldn't make a scene and ruin the family party, not when Ceinlys held all the cards.

It was one thing to feel stupid and used. Another to be jobless and unemployable.

She stared at the rows of expensive, overpowered cars in the lot. Mark had driven the two of them to the grove. Could she get a taxi back to the city? How, when she didn't even know the address of the Pryce family grove? She'd never be able to call for a cab.

Impatient, she looked around again. There had to be somebody out here. Then she saw a guy unlocking a red sports car. She ran toward him. "Wait!"

He got in his car.

"No! Wait!" She ran even faster and thudded into the passenger door. Her still numb fingers shaking, she yanked it open and climbed inside.

"What the hell?" he said.

"Are you going to the city?"

"What if I am?"

"Can you take me with you?" Desperate, she spoke fast. "You can drop me off anywhere in the city, so long as it's downtown."

He looked at her, and she took the opportunity to study him. He had the clean profile of the Pryce men. He wore a dark shirt and slacks that looked European, and his blue eyes held nothing but iciness. She got a feeling that he rarely if ever smiled. "You aren't one of the cousins," he said.

"I'm not a Pryce if that's what you're wondering."

"You look familiar though."

"Does that matter?"

He regarded her thoughtfully. "Seat belt."

She buckled in.

He started driving, never going over the speed limit. There was something very methodical about the way he maneuvered his car. Hilary finally noticed they were inside a Lamborghini. Who drove one like that? She stole a quick glance at him. She'd probably run into him at the party, even if she couldn't place him. There had been so many people.

Over an hour later, they reached L.A. She almost wept with relief at the familiar skyline. She was back where she was more comfortable. This was her city as much as Mark's, and she could take care of herself here.

"Thank you," she said finally. "I would've been stranded there without your help."

"I doubt that," he said. "You're Mark's Quarterly Girl. He would've given you a ride."

She choked down her humiliation. "That wouldn't have been a good idea."

"Get dumped already?"

Her jaw set at the casual way he asked the question. He didn't seem to mean it cruelly, but it was inconsiderate nonetheless. "Not exactly," she said, wishing time would speed up.

He snorted. "At this rate, we'll need to start calling his girlfriends Monthly Girls."

"That's not nice."

"Why not? Do I need to douse everything with sugar to make it more palatable for you?" He pointed out an old rusty Ford truck. "See that out there? Slapping a Ferrari logo on it won't make it a Ferrari. Just pathetic and contemptible."

Hilary started. This man saw everything in black and white. Was there anything in between? "Are you always this blunt?"

Nothing on his face changed. He was like a robot. "Usually. It saves time. Where do you want to be dropped off?"

She saw Galore. "This is fine." She could walk to anywhere she wanted to go from the sandwich shop.

The car stopped, and she got out. "Thanks."

"Good luck." The Lamborghini's blinker went on, and the car pulled smoothly back into traffic.

She couldn't stop the flow of tears as a fist closed around her heart. Luck wasn't something that would ever be hers.

WHERE WAS SHE?

Mark walked down the main path, looking around for Hilary. He'd tried her phone, but she hadn't answered. Maybe she couldn't get decent reception out here.

He saw Eliza walking toward him. She wore a strapless white top that had to have been chosen to avoid tan-lines. She hated them. Her pale blue skirt came down to mid-thigh, and for once she had put on a pair of sensible Converse sneakers. She waved. "There you are."

"Hey. I thought you were going to be here earlier."

"Yeah, I got held up. Why aren't you at the bar?"

"Don't even think about it. I already did my party trick for the event."

"Oh, no. I missed it?"

"Maybe next time. Hey, have you seen Hilary?"

"No." Eliza cleared her throat. "But since you brought her up, I have to say you were right about my event. I found out Taylor and her friends were talking trash about Hilary."

"Were they now." Mark ground his teeth. Maybe word had gotten back to Hilary somehow…that would explain her unhappy reaction after the charity dinner. Taylor could be vicious.

"Don't worry," Eliza said coldly. "I've already taken care of it."

"Thanks, doll. You're the best."

"Too true."

"Stop telling her that. She'll become completely unmanageable." Iain hugged her and gave Mark a fist-bump. "I was just looking for you."

"What's up?" Mark said.

"I saw Hilary leaving with Dane. Thought you should know."

With Dane? "You sure?"

"Only one person drives a red Lamborghini around here."

Mark cursed. Dane was the last person he wanted Hilary to get close to. Not that he was the type to poach or anything, but Dane was the least cheery person ever and had a bad habit of making every little issue sound ten times worse. If Dane talked about Mark, Hilary would run the other way screaming. "Thanks. Excuse me."

He found a secluded spot under a big twisted orange tree and called Hilary. She didn't pick up. Shit. Had Dane already scared her off? He dialed Dane's number, and thankfully his oldest brother answered.

"Dane Pryce."

"Hey, are you with Hilary?"

"You mean the Quarterly Girl?"

Mark's grip tightened around the phone. "She's my *girlfriend*."

"Not the impression I got."

"Is she there?"

"No."

"But she left with you, right? So where is she?"

"Don't blame me for your problems. Next time, dump your girlfriend after you take her home so I don't have to play chauffeur. Imagine if she'd been stuck out in bum-fuck orange-land with no car or a helpful stranger."

"You took her home?"

"She jumped into my car without even checking who I was. I'll tell you, she's lucky she didn't get in the car with somebody with less than kind intentions."

"You're anything but kind!" Dane was infamous for the ice in his veins.

"Yeah, yeah, and you're the sweetest guy ever. But she preferred me to staying with you." He hung up.

Mark sputtered. What the hell? What happened to make her think she was dumped?

He needed to see Hilary now and repair whatever damage had been done. He should've known better than to leave her side.

EIGHTEEN

ILARY RETRIEVED HER PRIUS FROM THE company garage. It was still where she'd left it the day she'd gotten too sick to drive home.

She fumbled at the door, got in, and took several deep breaths. Her heart galloped, her scalp felt vise-tight. She needed to calm herself down before she popped a vein. The only way Ceinlys could have found out about her past drug use was through Bebe. They'd done some wild things together when they were young, before Hilary's mom died.

As for the video and fake fiancée… Hilary tried to think it through. Why would anybody do that to her? Or was it about Walt? No…that didn't feel right. He didn't have any messed up past baggage out to sabotage him.

But she did. Her shoulders tight, she gripped the steering wheel until it started shaking. The muscles in her jaw creaked as her teeth clenched. Things had started to go bad around the time Bebe showed up. And that couldn't have been a coincidence.

Was this her cousin's twisted way of "improving" the situation? If she wanted to create a repeat of Freddie, she could've just seduced Walt. But after a moment's consideration, Hilary tossed the thought aside. Walt wasn't really rich, he wasn't hot and he certainly wasn't a bad boy. He wouldn't have appealed to Bebe in any way.

Furious, Hilary started driving to her aunt's place. Bebe was probably still there. Given how she had no interest in getting a job, she would stick around until she managed to find a guy she could ride for a while or get enough money to split again. That was Bebe's MO.

Hilary marched right into the house. Lila was seated on the sagging living room couch, the TV blaring some trashy show. A tearfully furious woman was screaming at a man and pushing him. Loud bleeps masked strings of four-letter words, and security men in dark uniforms joined the fray to separate the two before there was bloodshed. Lila's eyes were wide and bright as she absorbed the drama.

Hilary walked right past, momentarily blocking the TV, and Lila finally raised her head.

"Hilary? Are you all right?" she asked, searching Hilary's face.

"Is Bebe upstairs?"

"Uh-huh. You want me to get her?"

Hilary shook her head. "It's all right. You just watch your TV."

She went upstairs and debated. Would Bebe have taken over her room? That seemed likely given how much she wanted to take everything that belonged to Hilary.

Hilary opened the door to her room. Sure enough, her cousin was napping on her bed. dressed only in a threadbare tee-shirt and thong. The left side of her face was pressed against the pillows, and she snored softly, her mouth open and moist with drool.

Fury boiled up inside Hilary. This was what she would've become if she'd been like the rest of her family. Was this really how Bebe wanted to live the rest of her life? No job, no friends, nothing else to show for her time on the planet? She was only in her mother's home because she didn't have the money to take off to some *more fun* place.

Then again, maybe this was fun enough. Her idea of a good time was stirring up trouble and fucking with Hilary.

"Get up," Hilary said, smacking her cousin sharply on her bare leg. "Get up!"

Bebe started and opened her eyes blearily. "What—hey. What are you doing here?"

"This is *my* room," Hilary said.

"Thought you moved out to be with your fancy friend downtown. Not that I blame you. Jo's lookin' pretty good now." Bebe yawned and sat up. "What do you want?"

What did Hilary want? The question made her head throb. She'd had the most perfect speech prepared, but she couldn't remember a single word. So she latched onto the first thing Ceinlys had spoken of. "Did you hire an actress to play Walt's fiancée?"

Bebe shrugged with a bland look on her face. It was admission enough.

"Why did you do it?" Hilary forced the question out between clenched teeth. "Why?"

"For a girl who acts like she's all that, you sure are fucking stupid." Bebe hopped off the bed and brushed past Hilary to stand tall and straight, her eyes bright with defiance. "You dated him because you knew I'd never want to fuck a guy that dull."

"Are you insane? You've been gone for fifteen years! Not everything I do is about you."

"Yeah, it is. You and I are just like our mothers, okay? We have the same tastes, the same looks, and we wanna fuck the same kind of guys too. And I just know you weren't dating Walt for good sex. Ten to one he has a small dick."

Hilary's hands clenched, nails digging into her palms. "Did you film the whole thing and upload it?"

"Yeah. She said she'd give me a discount. I guess she really needed some exposure."

"Are you crazy?"

Bebe gave her a cockeyed grin. "Yep. Still the same, even after all these years."

"And did you tell Ceinlys about how we did ecstasy that time?"

"She asked if we did anything fun and wild. So yeah, why not? It's not like ecstasy is a big deal."

"It *is* a big deal. I could lose my job over it." Hilary's entire future could vanish because of a stupid mistake she'd made decades ago.

Bebe sneered. "Who gives a shit about the job? You have Mark, right? He's rich…and I'll bet he's good in bed."

Hilary's temples pounded. A thousand hammers beat in her head, all off-rhythm and horrendous. "What did you do?"

"What didn't I do?" Bebe smiled. "I told him everything. It's not like he's not going to find out soon enough. Told him how we were a combo deal. If he gets you, he gets me too. He knows we aren't just cousins, but practically sisters. Well. We are half-sisters. It's a fuckin' hot fantasy, Hilary. Every guy wants to fuck twins, and half-sisters who look like us is pretty close. Mark isn't any different."

One thing Bebe understood better than Hilary was the sordid nature of men. Hilary felt sick to her stomach. Everything she'd thought to be true was a lie. "How could you? How could you ruin my life? I thought he was different. I thought I had it made and that I could at least take care of myself instead of medicating myself to death like Mom!" Her mom hadn't cared about anything or anyone once Tim had been gone. She'd started with prescription meds, but when they hadn't been enough anymore, she'd started to experiment with crack. The end had come quickly after that.

"Don't be such a self-righteous cunt, okay? Why you gotta act so special? The way you go on, it's like you never had a dick shoved up your ass. You ain't that innocent. I know Freddie fucked you every way a guy can. He told me so. But you know what else he told me? He said you're a lousy lay because you just don't know how to let go. And you give a terrible blowjob."

Hilary jerked like she'd been struck. How could Bebe talk like this?

"What, you didn't know that?" Bebe continued in her high-pitched voice. "You honestly thought you were such hot shit? I'll bet when Mark fucked you, what he really fantasized about was me on my knees and taking him into—"

Heat seared through Hilary. "Shut up!" If she'd had a gun, she might have shot Bebe at that moment.

"—my mouth, all the way to my throat. He knows what I can do for him."

A curtain of red descended on Hilary's vision. She launched herself at Bebe, grabbing a fistful of her hair and yanking hard until Bebe fell.

Bebe screeched and elbowed Hilary's shin. Hilary hopped, lost her balance and landed on top of her cousin. One of the spaghetti straps on her dress broke; Bebe grabbed it and pulled, ripping the dress halfway down the bodice .

"Oh… My…!"

Both stopped at the breathless voice of Lila. Her eyes were as big as full moons, and they sparkled like they'd used to when Tim had been around.

My god. Lila's enjoying *this.*

Somebody stepped to the side from behind Lila. "Hilary?"

Her mouth dried at the sight of Mark. His jaw was slack, his eyes darting back and forth between her and Bebe.

We must be quite a spectacle. Rolling around on the floor with her cousin. Her hair was a mess now, her dress beyond repair.

Bebe started laughing. "Oh my god. Look at you. You're just a Rosenberg girl, not some special snowflake!"

Hilary had to get out before she did something she would regret. She kneed Bebe in the belly. When her cousin released her hair, she jumped to her feet and rushed out before Mark could regain his composure.

"Hilary, wait!"

She ran as fast as she could. Mark might be taller, but she had the advantage of a head-start. She hit *Unlock* on her car fob, hopped in and quickly locked the doors.

Mark came to a skidding halt and banged on the window. "Hilary!"

She gave him a daggered look. "I hate you," she said, over-enunciating each word so he would be able to make out what she was saying. "Don't bother me again."

Her gaze straight ahead, she started her car and sped off. She couldn't believe how easily she'd sunk to her cousin's level. How avidly her aunt had watched their sordid wrestling. If it hadn't been for Mark's presence, her aunt might have even started egging them on.

Tears spilled down Hilary's hot cheeks. Everything was over and Bebe was right. No matter how she tried, she couldn't escape her past.

MARK WATCHED HILARY'S BLUE PRIUS DISAPPEAR around the curve. His hands shook as he raked his hair. What the hell just happened? How in the world could things go this bad this fast?

"What are you doing, standing out here like an idiot?" Bebe said gleefully. "Did you see her run out? Like that would change anything. She's never gonna outrun her nature."

He turned around and saw her. Her shirt had a

rip, and she hadn't even bothered to put on pants. Christ. "Go inside and get dressed," he said tersely. He didn't even want to extend her that much courtesy, but she was still Hilary's cousin.

"Don't be like that." She gave him a sultry look. "You know you liked the show. Us, rolling on the floor like that? A little more time, I would've had her naked."

He stared at her with horror and disbelief. He felt sick inside. Were these the kind of people Hilary had grown up with? People who would do anything to bring her down?

Bebe rolled her hips as she came closer, then reached under the loose shirt she was wearing and cupped her breasts toward him. "Don't you want a little taste? They're real, and I always take good care of my girls."

"Get away from me before I call the cops."

"You'll be calling for help when I have your dick in my mouth." She licked her lips and gave him a wink. "Or maybe begging for mercy. I can suck it better than anybody. Better than that prude Hilary, that's for sure."

"You're a disgusting piece of work," he spat. "Stay away from me and Hilary."

Her eyes flashed, and she dropped her tits and put her hands on her hips. "Or what?"

"Or I'll make your life a living hell."

"You aren't the only one with money."

He looked at this trashy woman who felt no shame whatsoever standing in public virtually naked. "You have no money, and you have nothing to offer anybody. Who'd come to your rescue?" Then something clicked into the puzzle. "My ex, Taylor?" Bebe's face was blank. "My mom?" Ah, a slight tick under her left eye. He laughed. "Let me tell you a secret. Mom doesn't give a shit what happens to you. Mom only cares about us—her children—and she'd never side with you over one of her own." Ugly red blotches appeared on Bebe's face. Could she sense the truth of his words? God, he hoped so. "Leave L.A.," he said roughly. "I don't want to see your face ever again."

"You can't make me!" Her voice was shrill now. "You don't own this town."

He took a couple of steps toward her, towering over her and letting the intensity of his determination show through. "There are lots of ways I can force the issue—all legal, all draining and all humiliating for you. It wouldn't bother me at all to ruin you utterly. You won't be able to buy a cheeseburger without somebody hassling you. I'll make sure of it."

"I got no money," she whined.

"Guess you'll have to peddle your ass for gas money, then, huh? But I'm sure it won't be the first time."

He turned and left her there, striding away to his car. There had to be a way to fix this with Hilary. But first he needed to figure out exactly what had happened while he hadn't been watching.

NINETEEN

ARK PULLED OUT OF HILARY'S DRIVEWAY, speed-dialing his mother's number. She was the only one who could've turned what had started out as a great day into a total disaster. She wanted Hilary out of the way the most, didn't she? She'd even talked to Bebe, who was a pure viper.

"Hello dear," came his mother's soft voice. "Where are you? I've been looking for you."

"I'm in front of Hilary's home."

Ceinlys grew quiet. Then she said, "Did she want to leave so soon?"

Mark couldn't believe how innocent she sounded, like she didn't have the foggiest idea. "You made her go."

"I don't know what you mean."

"She left with Dane. I came after her."

"If she wants to go with Dane, let her. Come back to the party, Mark. Everyone misses you."

"I don't care about 'everyone.' I care about Hilary. You talked to Bebe, didn't you? What did you do to Hilary?"

Finally his mother said, "Bebe wanted to talk. She offered information in exchange for money, and she told me everything. It was quite a history that Hilary has. I was scandalized."

"How can you believe her? She's a liar."

"I expect so, a family like that. But Benjamin was able to corroborate everything."

Mark's gut grew icy. Benjamin Clark was a damn good PI. But why did Hilary's past matter? It wasn't like he was a pristine package himself. "She sold her cousin out."

"Yes. For fifty dollars."

"*What?*"

"I know, shocking."

It wasn't merely shocking. It was a what-the-fuck.

"Mark, dear, I don't understand what you expected. They're that sort of people. No loyalty or sense of duty to their family. Completely self-centered." Her sigh came low and clear over the line. "It's better this way…that she leaves before anybody gets hurt."

Hilary already seems pretty hurt. "Did you threaten her?"

"Of course not. I merely promised to release the information I was able to gather."

"Mother!"

"It's not the same thing, so don't you *mother* me. And if she hadn't done anything wrong, she wouldn't have run off. Did she cling to you? Beg you to shut me up and bail her out?" Ceinlys sounded reasonable and calm, like she'd expect Hilary to behave like that.

"I wish she had," Mark said. "Then I would know what to do. She won't even look at me anymore."

"It'll hurt a bit, but you'll get over it soon enough. If Katarina isn't to your taste, fine. Get yourself some young model or actress. It'll be therapeutic for you."

"How can you talk like that? Like they aren't even people?"

"The only thing that matters to me is my children and their happiness—*your happiness*." Ceinlys's voice turned hard. "The rest is irrelevant."

Mark hit the end button. He couldn't talk to her anymore without feeling sick. How could she think like that? How could she speak like stomping on others for his happiness was acceptable?

It might be his fault that she thought this. He'd certainly gone through his share of women, discarding them within three months, like it was nothing. He'd sampled one after another like desserts at a buffet. Why would his mother give them any more respect than he did?

He pulled over and pressed his forehead against the steering wheel, swallowing bitter bile. It *was* his fault that his mother thought the women he dated deserved about as much consideration as fruit flies because it wasn't just her. He'd been such a shallow ass that everyone sounded like they were reading from a shared script when they described his habits. Eliza had been spot-on when she'd threatened to call him Ken. He was about as real and heartfelt as that Barbie accessory.

The last thing Hilary needed was a man so screwed up he wouldn't know what genuine emotions were like even if they punched him in the gut. What could he possibly give her? Some fun time and laughs and then lots of heartache when he failed to meet her expectations for something true and lasting.

His father had been right all along. Maybe it would be better if Mark let go of Hilary the way Salazar had with his small-town mistress.

Mark gnawed on his knuckles, staring at the roadside. He had no idea where to go or what to do. He didn't want to go back to his penthouse, where Hilary's scent lingered.

Z, he thought. It was what he always did when he came out of a relationship. *I'll hit Z.*

The place was open. The only time it closed was Thanksgiving and Christmas. The Fourth of July should've been a slow day for the hip club, but it was crowded with people who didn't have anybody to spend the holiday with.

Sort of like him.

It felt nasty to be forced out of a relationship. Was this how his exes had felt when he'd ended things? He'd always given them expensive breakup presents, but they probably couldn't make up for the sour caustic feeling in their gut, like the one in his.

He ordered a whiskey and hit it hard. The bartender knew him and started a tab. Mark didn't even feel a buzz. The curse of his father's side of the family—everyone could drink like fish. It wasn't until he had five drinks that he started to get a mild buzz. It dulled the sharpness of the shards digging into his heart, but not by much. Suddenly there was a soft hand on his forearm.

"Mark, is that you?"

He looked up and grinned goofily. "Hey Zhara. What are you doing here? I thought you were in the Bahamas for a shoot."

"We finished early. So I am back."

Zhara no-last-name was a model from India. Tall, leggy and with skin the color of deep bronze, she was currently the flavor of the month in the world of fashion. There was something wholesome about her, but her large black eyes held just a hint of mischief that drew people to her. She looked around for an empty seat, and when there wasn't one, she sat in his lap and laughed. "Just imagine if my father saw a picture of this."

Mark chuckled. Her father was an ultra-conservative in India and disapproved of his daughter's career. That was probably why she had to disavow her family name. "You're a bad girl."

"I know. I surely deserve a spanking." In another woman it would have been a blatant come-on, but Zhara was a lesbian…another fact that might send her father into cardiac arrest if it ever came out. "So why are you drinking here alone? Where's your new girlfriend?"

"She…" Mark scowled into his once again empty glass. "She dumped me."

Zhara drew back with a look of humorous amazement. "No! Really? But how can… I mean, you *are* Mark Pryce."

"I guess she's immune to all that." More than immune. She was repulsed by so many things about him.

"Are you sure she's into men? I cannot imagine any red-blooded heterosexual woman not wanting you. You're gorgeous."

He chuckled humorlessly. "Now you're trying to flatter me out of the funk."

"Perhaps I am. Is it working?"

"Not really."

"Ah." Her shoulders drooped. "Well, what happened?"

"She doesn't want me. She thinks I'm the kind of guy who can't commit, and she thinks I'm going to ruin her life."

"There is some basis for this," Zhara said carefully. "I mean… She's only going to last three months with you."

"I've been watching her for close to a year now. The more I get to know her the more I want her."

She raised her perfectly plucked eyebrows. "Words I never thought to hear from you. Now I must hear more about this perfect woman."

"Well…she's great." Mark sighed and signaled for another drink. "She's beautiful, sexy, smart, dedicated, loyal, funny, stubborn, determined… She clawed her way out of a really bad situation—a really shitty childhood—and made something amazing of herself."

"She sounds incredible. Is she for real?"

"She is. I wouldn't change a thing about her."

"Are you in love with her?" Zhara asked, her eyes curious.

The bartender placed a new drink in front of him, and Mark took another long swig of the whiskey. "Maybe. I don't know."

"You sure? It sounds like love to me."

He shrugged. "It doesn't matter. She thinks I'm

a player. My father's son and all that, and so much more."

Zhara's expression softened. "You are your father's son, but that doesn't mean you are him."

"But what if I screw up? What if I make her unhappy or can't love her the way she deserves to be loved?" He slammed the glass down, sloshing the liquor. "If she changes for the worse because of me...I don't think I could stomach that." He didn't want to do to Hilary what his father had done to his mother.

"My friend, the fact that you're worried about it at all tells me you won't spoil this soup. Some people will delude themselves and think they're hot stuff when they're really just...idiots. You have seen this?"

He nodded.

"But they are not the people who care and want to do the right thing and worry about making mistakes. I think you'll make this paragon of womanhood very happy. You just have to convince her to take a chance on you if she's that skittish. But I have a feeling she will. What woman could resist you if you put your mind to it?"

He laughed. Somehow, Zhara's faith in him was pumping his confidence back up to its normal level. And she was right of course. He should take a chance. "You're so damn good for my ego." He hugged her.

Hugging him back, she planted a kiss on his cheek. "What are platonic friends for?"

Tossing his keys in a metal bowl he'd bought at an art auction a while back, Iain rolled his shoulders. It had been one long and less than successful family gathering. At least the cousins had stuck around even if Dane and Mark had bailed. Their mother had looked stony the entire time, and Iain was pretty sure it had something to do with Mark's date. Mom should've let them be. Mark's love life was his own, and he was old enough to know who he wanted to date.

Iain popped a beer can and sat back on his couch. It was late…but not too late to go out for a little clubbing. He clicked on the TV for an exciting round of channel surfing while he decided. Some music show was displaying a scantily dressed singer wriggling like her ass was on fire. Unfortunately, the wriggle was off beat.

His phone rang, and he picked it up. An unknown number. Huh.

"Iain Pryce," he answered.

"Iain, thank god," came a familiar voice. "It's Zhara."

"Hey. I had no idea you were in town. I would've made plans to hang out with you instead of watching a really bad singer trying to be a cheap stripper on TV."

"Can you come to Z?" She sounded harried and somewhat frazzled.

He frowned. "You there right now?"

"Yes, with a very drunk Mark. I don't think he can walk."

"I…too…walk!" came his younger brother's slurred voice.

Ah, jeez. "Okay. Give me fifteen minutes."

By the time he got there, Mark was slumped at the counter with Zhara watching him with her arms crossed. She looked stunning, like some exotic Indian goddess incarnate. Of course if he told her that, she'd laugh at him, which made her fun to hang out with. "What the hell?" Iain asked. "Mark never drinks more than he can handle."

"Apparently there is a woman he's in love with." She shook her head, and her loose brown-black curls bounced around her shoulders. "Can you believe it? Mark Pryce, finally fallen."

Iain shrugged. "It's about time I guess."

"You are still single."

"I'm old and set in my ways." Iain poked his brother. "Yo. Can you get up?"

Mark didn't move. "'*Course.*"

"Guess that's a no." Iain paid Mark's tab, then cleared a small space around the stool, bent down and carefully eased his brother into a fireman's carry. Mark made a vague sound of protest, but didn't resist.

Iain carried him out to the parking lot and dumped him in the passenger seat of his car. "Thanks for watching out for him, Zhara."

"No worries. Ring me sometime when you get a chance. We should hang out."

"Yeah, we should." He watched her disappear back into the club and felt a lopsided smile tug at his mouth. What a woman. Of course she wouldn't have been good enough for their mother either. Ceinlys seemed determined to marry them off to heiresses from only the most impeccable families...as if they needed the money. Besides, marrying within a few select families could have unintended consequences. Look at what had happened to the European royals.

He drove to Mark's penthouse and fished the keys out of his younger brother's pocket. He dragged Mark toward the master bedroom, but his brother stirred and said, very clearly, "No."

"What do you mean, no? You need to get some sleep."

Mark gestured at the couch.

"You'll be more comfortable in bed."

"Couch."

Shrugging, Iain dumped his brother where he wanted. "You gonna be okay by yourself?"

"Ung," Mark grunted, his face half-buried in sofa cushions.

"That really inspires confidence." Iain went to the bar and poured himself a finger of Laphroaig. His younger brother had really good stuff. Why hadn't he just stayed home and raided his own bar?

"Gimme." Mark extended a hand.

"Are you kidding? You're already too drunk."

Mark flexed his fingers.

"I feel like a bad influence." Iain handed Mark a glass of water. "There. If you finish that, I'll give you more."

Mark drank all of it and extended the hand again.

"Fine. Don't blame me if you feel like shit tomorrow." Iain gave him the bottle of whiskey. Watching his brother drink, Iain shook his head and walked away to the balcony before pulling out his phone. "Mom?"

"Iain. Do you know what time it is?" she said, her voice heavy with sleep.

"Yeah, I know. It's about Mark."

"What about him?" She sounded sharper now, more awake.

"He got badly drunk. I brought him home safe and sound, but somebody should check up on him tomorrow."

Ceinlys sighed impatiently. "I see."

"Mom, don't be so hard on him."

"I'm not. I'm disappointed. That's all."

"You know... He's been drinking because of Hilary."

"What did she do?" Ceinlys asked sharply.

"She left him."

A short pause. "Is that what he told you?"

"That's what his drinking buddy told me. Mark's a grown man. You shouldn't try to run his love life, trying to break up his relationship." He didn't need to have the whole scenario explained to know his mother had had a hand in the mess.

"It wasn't supposed to be this complicated." She sighed. "He wasn't supposed to care."

"I think he really loves her."

"But why *her*, Iain?" She sounded confused, like somebody had told her the sky was actually green. "She's not even all that pretty. I don't understand what the attraction is."

"Well... Can anyone really understand what's in someone else's heart? He likes her. Isn't that enough?"

"He think he wants her now, but... They're going to end up hurting each other. There simply isn't enough to hold them together."

Iain dug his fingers into the back of his neck.

"She's older than he is," Ceinlys continued. "Not that well educated. He'll lose interest soon enough, and regret he ever tried to convince anybody he really cared for her."

"If he changes his mind, I'm sure he'll leave her." But Iain had a feeling Mark wouldn't. This wasn't just another of his infatuations. He knew his brother, and could tell that he hadn't approached Hilary on impulse, or just to avoid getting set up with Katarina, no matter what he said.

"No, he won't." Words tumbled out quickly over the phone line. "He'll stay out of some misplaced sense of pride. He'll stay because he's told everyone she was different…that she was somehow special. But he'll be miserable, and he'll stray. When she finds out—and she will inevitably find out—she'll be hurt, then angry…then miserable and desperate. She'll try to change him, until one day she realizes she can't. Then they'll both be old, and remain together simply because that's what they know and are comfortable with." Ceinlys sniffled.

"Mom…"

"I don't want any of you to be unhappy. I want all of you to have the kind of contentment your father and I never had."

"Mark isn't just Dad's son," Iain said quietly. "He's your son too."

He heard tears on the other side. "Of course he's my son. All of you are mine."

Iain rubbed his chest, that particular spot that never really stopped aching. "Have faith, Mom."

TWENTY

O N SUNDAY AFTERNOON, HILARY SAT IN JO'S condo and went through a list of rental possibilities while Jo commented. "I don't know. That's a convenient location, but the buildings are pretty shitty. Amandine's assistant used to live in the neighborhood."

"But it's really cheap," Hilary said. "And available immediately."

"True." Jo cradled her chin in her palm. "What's the deal here, though? You seemed okay with living with your aunt. What's this urgency with looking for a new place?"

"I can't do it anymore. I just… I don't think it's good for me to be there. It's so full of my past. It ties me to it."

Hilary had already gone through and crossed out most of the listings since the disastrous Fourth of July. Mark thankfully hadn't tried to call her. But then he probably saw no reason to fake an interest in her when she knew what was really going on. For all she knew he was now in bed with Bebe, doing the same things he'd done with her.

She took a deep breath. She needed to stop or she'd get sick and start crying again. Jo had been out until Saturday evening and missed most of the tears, thankfully.

So yes, Hilary had been stupid…again. She'd made herself believe…and hope. But no more. Mark didn't deserve another bit of her mental energy. She had to harden her heart and move on if she wanted to survive this.

"You okay? You seem really odd ever since you went to that family party with Mark. Was anybody there nasty to you or something?" Jo asked.

"Nasty? No. It was more like…instructive. I was able to see how things are quite clearly." She needed to cut all ties with her past if she wanted to move on. If she hadn't been living with her aunt, would Bebe have been able to find her again so easily?

The only thing Hilary refused to do was leave the city. L.A. was her home, and she wasn't going to flee her friends or her job. She was going to do whatever she could to hold onto those—sometimes, they were all that kept her sane. And she needed them now more than ever before to remind herself she was not like Bebe or her mom or aunt.

"How about this one?" Jo said, pointing at a complex about thirty minutes away from the OWM headquarters. "This isn't too expensive, and it's been newly renovated. And they seem okay with pets, in case you want to get one."

Hilary snorted. "You think I'm going to be a cat lady?"

"Or a dog, but dogs are pretty high maintenance. You have to walk them and stuff."

"Working for Gavin keeps me plenty busy. I don't think I need to add more to my life."

Jo frowned, then sighed, then opened her mouth, then closed it. Hilary scrawled *GP* for "good possibility" across the apartment listing and said, "What? Just say it."

Jo sighed again. "Mark called me."

Hilary tensed. "What did he want?"

"He wanted to know where you were, so…I said you were staying with me."

"That's all?"

"Yeah."

"Wonder why he bothered. It can't be to send me bribes." Tim had always brought gifts to smooth things over when he'd screwed up. Her mother had forgiven him for the price of a cheap box of chocolates, but Hilary wouldn't bend for something that ridiculous. Nothing would change her mind, not even the most ostentatious yacht in the world. She would never be with a guy who could jeopardize her financial security and independence.

"He sounded pretty bad. Come on. I can sense this weird vibe from you. And him too. It was so palpable I could feel it over the phone."

Hilary closed her laptop. "Ceinlys threatened to get me fired."

"What?" Josephine laughed her signature "what an idiot" laugh. "Gavin would never fire you. And he doesn't even like her."

"That's not the point. She found out that I lied on my job application."

That wiped out the mirth from Jo's face. "You did?"

"Yeah. It asked if I had ever done any drugs, and I said no."

"And this is a problem because…?"

"I was, uh, a little wild when I was younger. And there were a few times when I did some ecstasy with Bebe when we were out clubbing."

"Well, yeah, okay. But you aren't doing it now, are you?"

"Oh, hell no. I haven't touched anything like that for years." Hilary had lost the stomach for it after her mom died of overdose.

"See? He's not going to get rid of you over something that happened like forever ago. I bet the statute of limitations has run out."

"He wouldn't want to, but he'd have to. You remember about seven months ago, he fired three people from the firm?"

Jo frowned slightly. "I think I heard something about that."

"They lied on their application. So he fired them, even though they were really good at their jobs. He said the firm won't tolerate people who can't be honest."

"Oh shit."

"Ceinlys promised to locate them and have them sue for wrongful termination and discrimination if he didn't fire me. He wouldn't be able to win the lawsuit, and it would cost him lots of money and bad publicity. He'd *have* to let me go."

"God. She's such a bitch. But how did she find out? You didn't get busted or anything, did you?"

"Of course not. If I had, it would've shown up during the background check. Bebe spilled the beans."

Jo slapped the tabletop. "I knew she was trouble!"

"Well, yeah." Hilary took a deep breath. Suddenly she couldn't keep it inside anymore. "And that's not all."

"What else did she do?"

"You remember that whole thing with Walt's fiancée?"

"The 'News at 11' incident? Kind of hard to forget."

"Yeah, well, that wasn't his fiancée. It was an actress Bebe hired. She promised to film it and put it on YouTube for exposure, and the actress went for it. She faked the whole thing."

"Oh. My. God!"

"I know. And I was so furious and nasty to Walt." Hilary buried her face in her hands. "I owe him an apology." And the heirloom bracelet. She'd called him a few times, but he hadn't answered. Either he was unavailable or just really pissed off at her. Probably both. It wouldn't surprise her if he tried to sue her like she'd dared him to. She'd messed everything up.

"Do you want me to kill her? Because I will. For free!"

"Don't. I should thank her in a way."

"How?"

"She helped me see how stupid I was about Mark."

"What did he do?"

"He knew."

"What?"

"He knew everything about my mom, aunt, Tim and Bebe and Freddie. She went to his restaurant and told him everything. Apparently this happened in his private office, and knowing Bebe, I can only imagine what she offered him in addition to the story."

"Eww," Jo said, scrunching her face.

Hilary rubbed her temples. "When I confronted her, she said she'd proposed a threesome." She sniffed and blinked away the tears. She'd shed plenty already. "What man wouldn't want to do it with twins? It's such a typical fantasy, you know? And Bebe and I are basically sisters. We have the same father and our mothers share the same DNA, so we're pretty close to that little male fantasy. And we look alike. Why wouldn't Mark be tempted?"

"Oh come on, Hilary. Surely Mark can't be that bad."

"I think he can be that bad. He ignored me for days until he and Bebe had a chat. After that it was all solicitousness and sweetness. I thought…" She started when a tear landed on her hand. Impatient, she wiped her cheeks. "I thought he was real. I thought he wasn't like other guys." She swallowed a sob. "I thought he was different."

"Oh hon." Jo pulled her into a big hug. "I'm so sorry."

"I wanted him to be different," Hilary sobbed, unable to hold it together in the face of her best friend's understanding and sympathy. "I wanted it so bad I got stupid about it. I should've known better. I'm not a good judge of men."

"Don't be so hard on yourself, Hilary. None of us can read people's minds. If Mark screwed you over, it's on him. He's the bad guy, not you." Jo pulled back and handed Hilary a tissue. "Life's unfair and shitty from time to time, but look at the bright side. You have a job. And Ceinlys probably won't follow through on her threat if you aren't seeing Mark. Everyone knows all she wants is to marry him off to some snotty heiress she found. You and Mark just weren't meant to be. But there's some other guy out there, waiting for you. And hey, you always have me. I don't care what happened when you were growing up. You're always going to be my best friend, and I'll always be there for you."

Hilary sniffled and wiped her face. "Thanks. You're the greatest friend anybody could ask for."

"I know," Jo said, making Hilary laugh. "Now let's forget all about that jerk and have some ice cream. I got five flavors in the fridge."

"WHAT IN THE NAME OF HEAVEN *IS* THIS SMELL?"

"Agh." Mark squeezed his eyes shut as bright light flooded the room. He kept his head down so it wouldn't fall off his neck and waved a hand feebly. "Hi, Mom," he mumbled into the couch pillow.

"Good god." He sensed his mother walking

around the living room floor of his penthouse. "Did you drink all this?"

"Think so." Iain had helped him with the whiskey over the last two—or was it three?—days, but Mark didn't think his brother would appreciate being ratted out. A lot of things were sort of fuzzy right now.

He felt a warm, soft hand on his face and an instant later smelled his mother's signature Chanel No. 5. "Do you need to go to the hospital?" she asked gently.

"No. I'll be fine."

"Someone who is fine does not keep his face buried in cushions or smell as rank as you." Ceinlys sighed and helped him up. "Come on. Sit up."

His head felt like it'd split in half, but worse than that was the way he felt inside. He wished he could throw up, but that wasn't the problem. The problem was that Hilary had eviscerated him. Just cut him wide open and ripped out everything inside him and deemed him unworthy.

"What's wrong?" she asked, cradling his head in the crook between her shoulder and chest. "Talk to me. I'm here for you."

"It's Hilary." He felt his mother tense underneath him. "People just hated her for being with me." He squinted up at his mother. She was still as beautiful as ever, but she looked so tired despite the smooth skin and artful makeup. He sort of wished he could go back to the simpler times, when he'd just been a child, unaware of life's problems. There was a reason why people said ignorance was bliss.

"I don't think Hilary is the kind of woman you want to be with for any long period of time. She's not like us. Did she tell you about her boyfriend's fiancée?"

"No."

"She was a hired actress."

His head was so stuffy, Ceinlys sounded like the teacher from old Charlie Brown cartoons he used to watch. Finally his brain registered her words, and he scowled. "What? Who hired her?"

"From what I gathered, Hilary's cousin."

His jaw slackened. "But why?"

"I don't know, but that isn't important. Hilary managed to use that to gain your sympathy, and you started going out with her so that she could save face."

He pinched the bridge of his nose. "That's not true. I'd been interested in her for a while. I just never had a good excuse to get, you know…personal. Besides, she didn't know I was coming by, so she couldn't have possibly staged it to get my attention."

Ceinlys blinked. "I see." Then she frowned. "But do you really want to be with her? She's not like us, Mark."

He chuckled dryly. "And what about me? I'm no prize."

"Don't you dare say that," she said sharply. "You're worth a thousand of her."

"Net worth, maybe. But I've never been able to maintain interest in a woman for very long...always seems like I get itchy and have to move on to somebody new. For all we know, I might have inherited Dad's temperament." His mother's lips firmed, but this close, he could see the small tremor in her jaw. "I'm sorry. I'm not trying to hurt you."

"I'm not hurt." She blinked a few times, very rapidly. "I'm surprised to hear you compare yourself to your father."

"Well, is it so unlikely? He can never be faithful to anybody. He couldn't change for you, or for that other woman..."

"You mean Blaine's mother."

He nodded.

"I thought perhaps he might," Ceinlys said. "I've never seen your father like that about a woman. I was so scared he'd discard me like trash...and after I'd given him five children! So I got myself"—she bit her lower lip—"never mind. It isn't important. I just want you to know you aren't like your father. You've always been a sincere and earnest boy. You don't look at women like they were just...playthings for you to enjoy and then toss aside when you get bored. You were never that cruel. I've seen you."

"Then why do I leave them within three months? People call them the Quarterly Girls. Did you know that?"

"I didn't, but what of it? You're still young. You haven't found the right woman yet, and you're paying for your father's past. Do you think anybody would've named your girlfriends that way if your father weren't what he is? Look at people like Jacob Lloyd. A bigamist and a horrible womanizer, but nobody has anything clever or cruel to say about any of that because his father wasn't like yours."

The thought stunned him slightly, but she was right. Jacob was the biggest jerk in recent history. But nobody had called him on his behavior. He'd come from a tight family.

"What's so special about Hilary?" Ceinlys asked.

"She just makes me want to do better. Every time I think about her, I can't help but smile. And I can't stop thinking about her."

"Do you love her?"

He considered, giving the question the weight it deserved. What he felt for Hilary extended beyond what he'd told his mother. There was bone-deep satisfaction and rightness when he made Hilary happy. He suffered so damn much when she was hurting. It was like he was born to cherish her. And no matter how scary it was, there was only one word to describe it: love. "I do."

Her eyebrows pinched, and deep lines appeared between them. "I never wanted that for you. Love, I mean."

"Mom!" Mark wasn't sure how he'd thought the conversation would go when Ceinlys had walked into his place, but this definitely wasn't it. "Why the hell not?"

"The simplest happiness in life is the most difficult to attain. I didn't want you to struggle for an impossible dream. It's always easier to have stability. It may be boring, but at least it doesn't disappoint you."

Mark hurt at the old pain in her voice. It was like those long-ago memories from his childhood, the hazy happiness that had disappeared layer by layer as the truth of his parents' marriage gradually became clear. It seemed so obvious now, why his mother wanted him to date socially acceptable heiresses. She wanted him to find some level of contentment in his private life. "I don't know if it's something I can have, but I want to try. I don't want to settle." He sat up and looked into his mother's beautiful eyes. "I know you threatened to get her fired. Will you please not do that? Her job's really important to her...and what's important to her is important to me, too."

"Of course." She took a shuddering breath. "I just want you to have a life that's better than mine."

"Thanks, Mom." Suddenly feeling light, he hugged her. "I love you, and I promise I will."

"See that you do. Now," Ceinlys said, her voice brisk and back to normal, "you must clean this pig sty. How can you even think of bringing a girl over here, especially one you love?"

TWENTY-ONE

FTER HIS MOTHER LEFT, MARK DOWNED four aspirins with some water and stared at his place. There were empty whiskey bottles all over the floor, fast food cartons on the table, a mass of something that had once been food on his kitchen counter...and one of his lamps was sitting in the closet for some reason. He gathered up the cartons, but when he opened the lid to the large kitchen garbage bin, a stench emerged that smelled like a pack of rotting zombies.

He quickly closed the lid and tilted his head back, breathing through his mouth. *Okay*, he thought, looking at the ceiling and panting slightly, *consuming alcohol clearly is not going to help me win Hilary back*. And he was going to win her even if he had to move heaven and earth.

He'd do anything to show her he wasn't like her dad or ex-boyfriends.

First to-do item: putting in a priority call to the maid service. Then he showered, got dressed and went to the new restaurant site. He had a meeting with the chef there—André—and he was late. Neglecting his businesses wouldn't show Hilary he was the kind of good, stable guy she wanted to be with. So he'd take care of that while coming up with a strategy to win her.

André harrumphed when Mark finally showed up. A stolid Frenchman of medium height with cropped black hair and a nose like an eagle's beak, André's complexion was always ruddy under a thin layer of fashionable stubble. They talked over the few items left to discuss before the restaurant's opening, but Mark couldn't keep his mind off Hilary. How she'd looked while she'd sampled the food he'd been considering serving. How—

"You seem distracted," André said.

"It's nothing."

The chef leaned close and sniffed. "Alcohol, both old and new. Must be a woman problem."

Mark winced. "Is it that obvious?"

"When men drink too much, there are two reasons. He has lost all his money or it is an *affaire de coeur* gone bad."

"Yeah. Well." Mark cleared his throat. "It's complicated."

"*Mais non*. Nothing is complicated in *amour*.

What you need to do is show her what's in your heart. See how easy that is?"

"I would if I could." He'd pay hundreds of millions of dollars if there was an X-ray machine that could show Hilary what she meant to him.

André chuckled. "Americans. They think too hard about such simple things. Cook for her! Nothing says *amour* like good food that you make with your own hands for a special woman."

"I don't cook," Mark said.

"Then perhaps you must learn."

Mark worried his lower lip. He'd never cooked for anybody. He'd always taken them to restaurants. On the other hand, André might have a point. There was a reason why people focused on food as the basis for human relationships, warmth and love, things that everyone longed for. "What should I make?"

"Something that reflects everything you feel about her. Sublime and true and honest and passionate, yes?" The Frenchman dug through a big folder and pulled out a few sheets. "Ah! I made these for a lover in Paris." He leaned in again. "And if I may confide... The sex afterward? *Formidable!*"

Mark winced inwardly. TMI. He took a look at the recipe, which was a mass of scribbled French. Crap, everything looked pretty complicated. But would a burger and fries—something he could probably manage without too much trouble—convince Hilary he was serious about her? Any guy could make her a burger. Even Walt had probably done that...so Mark was going to do better. "Fine. Let's try this one."

And for the next five hours, Mark slaved away in the kitchen under André's tutelage. The psycho Frenchman was convinced he couldn't use the same knife to chop up poultry and veggies, and everything had its own...whatever. Mark was thirsty, sweaty and tired, and he acquired a new burn on his forearm. The food had better be good.

André took one look at what was on the plate and sighed. "Fit only for pigs." He took a tiny piece and tasted it. "*Mais non*. Not even pigs."

"You're not being helpful."

"Cooking is about the heart, not just chopping meat and vegetables."

"Don't forget slicing," Mark added dryly. "Maybe this isn't going to work. I need something simpler."

"Simpler will not help. Practice will."

"I don't have the time." Mark took a bite of his own food, then made a face. André was right about it not being fit for anyone's consumption, especially Hilary's. "But cooking is a great idea, just not"—he gestured at the stuff on the counter—"this."

André shook his head, but Mark ignored him. Cooking *was* probably a great idea. He'd seen some romantic comedies where women liked that. And what had his mother said? Something about the simplest happiness. Why would that require a complex recipe invented by a French chef?

He considered… None of the people he knew could show him how to cook something simple and good. Except his half-brother Blaine. He used to run a bar and restaurant, and from what Mark had heard, he was a mean cook. And probably a better teacher than André.

"Now you are trying to find the easy way."

Mark started. "What?"

André gave him a look down the impressive length of his nose, somehow managing to seem both arrogant and friendly. "You are like new students at culinary school. Always looking for the easy way. *Mon ami*, there is no easy way. If she means so much to you, you'll learn. Otherwise you won't. Anything worth having requires work. Especially a woman. If she's not worth the work"—André gestured at the messy kitchen—"then maybe you should let her go, eh? Why do this for only a cheap hamburger and hot dog girl?"

André had a point, even if it was one Mark didn't like. "Fine. But you gotta teach me fast. I've got a deadline to meet, and I don't know exactly when it is. I just know it's close."

Hilary went to work extra early on Monday in her most conservative outfit and shoes—sensible and utterly boring pumps—and waited for Gavin to show. Since she'd broken things off with Mark, Ceinlys should be happy, but the woman had called Hilary twice since Sunday.

She'd left a message before hanging up: *Call me.*

What did that mean? Was that a good or bad omen?

Hilary rubbed her temples. She couldn't decide anymore. It was as if her ability to think had disappeared when Ceinlys had issued the threat. This was the price Hilary paid for her stupidity.

She tensed when Gavin appeared. He looked unusually perturbed. Had Ceinlys broken her promise to leave Hilary alone and spoken with him anyway? Was she going to be fired?

"Good morning," Hilary said, her mouth dry.

"Hi, Hilary. How are you feeling?"

"I'm fine, thanks."

"Good. Send the itinerary for the week to my tablet."

"Yes, sir." When Gavin disappeared into his office, she closed her eyes, her shoulders sagging. Maybe his less than chirpy mood was due to something else. The currency markets might have taken a dive over the weekend. Who knew?

She gripped her mug and read out loud, "A

Woman Worth Her Weight in Gold." That still had to mean something, right?

When she got a free moment, she called Ceinlys and reached her assistant instead. Hilary left a simple message: *You won. I've done everything you asked me to. Please don't call me again.*

"Really? I'm to tell Ceinlys exactly that?" the assistant confirmed, sounding somewhat skeptical and surprised.

"Yes. That's all. Thank you."

There was nothing more to say. Hilary had lost. She wasn't even going to pretend otherwise.

She continued to monitor Gavin's mood, but he didn't seem to treat her any differently. Her coworkers were as friendly as usual, and she hadn't received a single call from Ceinlys in the past four hours.

So far so good.

By Wednesday, she realized she'd been paranoid for nothing. Why wouldn't Ceinlys keep her word? She'd probably called Hilary to make sure she wouldn't latch onto Mark again or something. Now that she and Mark were through, Ceinlys's interest in Hilary was probably also in the past tense. The YouTube video was still up, but there was nothing to be done about that.

About a quarter till noon, Hilary left the office and went to Galore. The owner greeted her with a big smile, and she found comfort in the familiarity of the routine. She ordered her usual, a BLT, with an extra large latte. The caffeine would be necessary to fortify herself for the meeting that was about to happen.

After she got her lunch, she looked around. Walt was there as scheduled, at a small table near the window. Unlike the last time, he looked perfectly presentable and doctor-like in a pair of rimless glasses and heavily starched white button-down shirt. He'd also grown a goatee, which somehow suited him.

She went over and took the other seat at his table. "Hey."

"Hey," Walt said, his face unreadable. "So you changed your mind about the bracelet?"

"Yeah." She was pretty sure he wouldn't have made the time in his busy schedule to see her otherwise. She pulled out a jewelry box from her purse and handed it to him. "Here."

He opened the lid to check, then put the bracelet into his jacket pocket, sliding the box back to her side of the table. "Thanks," he said, looking past her.

"Walt… I owe you an apology."

"Do you?"

"Yes. I learned recently that that woman wasn't your fiancée after all. I'm sorry I was so nasty to you."

He shrugged carelessly, but the skin around his

eyes was still tight. "Any woman in your situation would've done the same."

"Maybe, but you deserve someone who would have believed you when you said you didn't know her." Hilary played with a fry. "I don't think I'm that woman for you."

"Are you saying this because you found some-body better? Mark Pryce, right? Rich guy...not like me with my huge med school debt." His face was hard. She'd never seen him like this before. He had always been so sweet and gentle. It came with his job.

Hilary put her fry down and lowered her gaze, unable to look at him. It was obvious how she'd wronged him. She should never have tried to use him to compensate for other men's mistakes. Walt deserved so much more than somebody like her. Maybe it was karma that her relationship with Mark had blown up in her face. "No. I don't think Mark and I are going to be able to work out our problems. He and I are too different. This is about you and me, Walt. We were always missing something. I don't know... Chemistry or sizzle or something."

"You think our relationship isn't worth fighting for because we don't have animal attraction?" Walt asked quietly.

"No. It's me. I've been using you in my own way to run away from my past. It was doomed from the very beginning. I'm so sorry, Walt."

"Well." He finished his coffee, his fingers rigid around the mug. "At least you're eager to analyze. You could've just said, 'It's not you, it's me.'"

"Walt…"

"Forget it. I just wanted the bracelet back." He got up and left, leaving her alone in the sandwich shop. She watched him disappear into the crowd.

It hurt to realize she was losing Walt. Not because she loved him. She knew she never had. But Walt was a nice guy, and now somebody she could've been friends with was opting out of her life.

Mark had ruined her, and she might never rebound.

TWENTY-TWO

"**H**ILARY, CAN I SEE YOU FOR A SECOND?" Gavin asked over the intercom the following Monday.

"Sure."

"I left the Morning Star fund papers at home. Do you mind picking them up?"

"Now?" she asked.

"Yup."

She frowned. She didn't remember Morning Star being so time sensitive. On the other hand, he was the financial genius, not her.

"Thomas will drive you," Gavin continued.

"He will?" This was getting a bit freaky. Thomas's duties didn't include chauffeuring her around.

"Otherwise you won't be able to unlock the gates," he said. "Just bring the documents a little after lunch, and that should be fine."

"Okay." She grabbed her purse and saw Thomas in front of the building, impeccably dressed as usual in a crisp dark suit. He opened the door to Gavin's Bentley, and she climbed in.

"Sorry about the bother," she said.

"No problem," Thomas said politely. He put in almost as many hours as Gavin, but he didn't seem to mind at all. Knowing Gavin, Thomas was probably extremely well-compensated for his time.

She leaned back, doing her best to relax. Gavin was sending her to his home. He wouldn't have done that if he was about to fire her.

Thomas drove past the gates, and Hilary couldn't help admiring her boss's gorgeous mansion. It could've been completely ostentatious. And it had been until Gavin had bought it. Now, she knew, it had such personal touches, especially after his wife had redone many of the rooms, that it felt sweetly homey…albeit in a billionaire style.

Before she got out, Thomas said, "Everyone's gone today. So you can just go in."

She nodded and slipped inside the house. The mansion smelled like thick wine sauces and meat— probably from an earlier meal, although the housekeeper generally cooked simpler Latin American dishes. A few colorful Lego blocks dotted the otherwise pristine marble floor, and she smiled to herself. Not even an army of staff could keep up with her boss's child.

She climbed the stairs to Gavin's home office. Hilary knew the interior layout intimately since she'd spent hours hammering out the details with the architect and builders every time Gavin was too busy to deal with them. She saw a big manila folder on his desk, opened it to make sure it was the right documents, and then started back.

Her neck prickled as she reached the first floor. She sniffed, then tilted her head. The heady scent had grown stronger. What was going on?

Then she heard metal clanging and a loud male curse from the kitchen. She peeked in, and her entire body stiffened at the sight of a familiar handsome face.

Mark.

What was he doing here? She stood under the arch between the kitchen and living room, frozen and uncertain. This was precisely the kind of situation she *shouldn't* be in if she wanted to keep her job. If Ceinlys found out, she'd consider it an act of war. Besides, it wasn't like Mark and Hilary had anything left to talk about.

Quietly, she took a step back.

"Hilary, come on into the kitchen," he called out. She hesitated.

"I know you're out there. Come on. I don't bite, and Mom doesn't know I set this up. If you don't come to the kitchen now, I'm going to make a huge scene."

"Nobody's here to see it," she called out.

"Which is why I'll put it on YouTube. There're a couple of cameras rolling right now."

Her entire body clenched. "That's blackmail!"

"True," he said, sounding entirely too comfortable with the idea.

Eyes narrowed, she marched into the kitchen, looking around for the cameras and keeping her gaze on anything but Mark. A mountain of copper pots and pans sat in the double sinks. Things were bubbling, sizzling and simmering on the stove, and a huge stack of vegetables, fresh herbs and meat sat on the counter. What was the point of all this stuff? He didn't cook.

Finally curiosity got the best of her. "What is all this?"

"Our lunch," he said. "And thank you for finally acknowledging my presence here."

She felt her cheeks heat. "Did you plan this?"

"Basically. I told Gavin I really needed to see you."

"I don't see any cameras."

"They're there. Gavin's home security system."

Hilary sat on the stool and shook her head. Her heart hammered in sharp beats. Why was he doing this? If this was some kind of cruel trick, she didn't think she could stand it. He'd already broken her heart. He didn't have to grind what was left under his heel. "I should've known something like this was going on. It was just too weird that Gavin wanted me to get his documents personally. Usually he asks Thomas for that."

Mark snorted. "I wasn't going to slave away for hours for Thomas." His forearms sported some burns that she didn't remember. Some of them looked a few days old. A couple of Band-Aids were wrapped around his left index and middle fingers. He looked like he'd gone through some kind of culinary war.

"Do you need help?" she asked to be polite. Maybe that would earn her enough brownie points to leave.

"Nope," he said. "Sit and relax."

So she did. He focused intensely, checking numerous kitchen timers, chopping vegetables, stirring sauce pans, inspecting whatever was in the oven and shaving white truffles. She couldn't believe he'd done all this. He'd told her he didn't cook for anybody. Why had he bothered?

Finally, he served their lunch. The sauce looked really good—thick and glazy over some kind of poultry, and she waited for him to set the table. He placed a big basket of bread in the center, and she asked, "Did you bake this?"

He shook his head grimly. "On top of all this other stuff? No."

She wanted to reassure him that it was fine, but kept silent. She didn't understand his end game. And to make matters worse, they were being filmed.

No. *She* was being filmed. Mark didn't count since it was his own doing.

Finally he sat down, and she studied the food. It looked really, *really* good, like something she might get from a high-end French restaurant.

"It's duck. André's super-secret recipe," he explained. "Slow-roasted for half a day. Try it."

Silently, she cut a small piece and sampled it. The meat itself was tender and juicy, but it was sort of bland, and the taste of thyme was slightly overwhelming. Then there was the sauce. It wasn't bad, but it was definitely missing something. Not truffle, since he had put a diamond ring's worth into the dish.

Mark's face slowly scrunched up as he chewed, and he put down his fork.

"What?" Hilary asked.

"I thought I got everything right this time." He pulled out his tablet and scrolled. She could guess how long and complicated the recipe must be given that it came from one of his French chefs and the pots and pans that towered behind him. He swore. "I forgot the kosher sea salt for the sauce."

"It's still good," she said, trying to make him feel better.

"And I forgot to add the port!"

"If we still have it, we should drink it."

"No, it's just cooking port." Mark dug his fingers into his eyes. "André said he wouldn't even feed my stuff to his pigs."

Hilary laughed. "Really?"

"Yeah."

"Well, I like it." Maybe it wasn't as perfect as what André might have made, but it was still pretty good.

"No, don't eat that."

"Oh stop. I'm not going to grade you or anything. Can we just eat? I only have an hour for lunch."

Mark said nothing, and he didn't eat that much. Maybe his refined palate couldn't take it. Well, whatever. It was good enough for her.

"You know, I appreciate what you've done," Hilary said. "But you shouldn't have. This is a pointless gesture. It's over." *I loved you, and all you wanted from me was the cheap thrill of a ménage a trois.* She could never say the words. Saying them out loud would give them too much power.

"If you're worried about my mom, don't. I talked to her, and she won't get you fired or anything like that."

"You…talked to her?"

"Yeah."

"When?"

"Last week. I know she can be a little scary, but really, it's okay."

"Well… Thank you," Hilary said, oddly touched and grateful he'd spoken to Ceinlys on her behalf.

"And Bebe's gone too. I made sure of it."

She looked away. "You don't have to fight my battles for me. I can take care of myself."

"Hilary, I swear to you, nothing happened between me and Bebe. I should've told you she came by, but I just didn't think it was important. I don't want her—*never* wanted her—and couldn't care less what you might have done in the past. That's not important to me. It has no bearing on how I feel about you."

She shook her head. He had to stop saying all the right things. She couldn't gamble on words alone.

"I want us to be together," he said.

"I don't."

"Why not? We get along great. We have fantastic chemistry. People would kill for that. I've never felt this way about anybody. I love you."

I love you. Those three precious words from the man who had so much power over her already. Freddie had been an arrow shot from a bow. Mark was a thermonuclear warhead. He could utterly destroy her, beyond repair, and she couldn't risk that much. Her heart bled again, and she bit her lower lip. Would the pain ever stop? "I can't be with a man whose feelings I can never be certain of."

"Hilary—"

"You feel like we have something special going on right now, but you'll change your mind soon enough. You think you want me because you don't have me. But once you have me back in your life, how long will it be before buyer's remorse sets in? I don't want that."

"I'm not the Mark who had girlfriend after girlfriend. I don't do Quarterly Girls anymore."

"Don't you? Can you really give them up?" Hilary looked at him, her body tight and shaky. "I don't think you can. We do have great chemistry, but I need more than that. I'm not some twenty-something girl trying to have a little fun. I need to be certain that the man I'm with is going to be true to me for the rest of our lives."

Suddenly Mark's jaw slackened. "So that's why you left. You wouldn't have dumped me over Mom's threat if you'd been sure I wouldn't move on to another woman. You think I'm going to be just like my dad." He leaned forward and looked into her eyes. "Well, you're wrong. You're not your mother, and I'm not my father. I can change."

"Yes, but I *have* changed. You haven't. You were out with a model just a few days ago at Z. I remember seeing her in *Vogue*."

He looked momentarily confused. "You mean Zhara? She's just a friend."

"Who was sitting on your lap, hugging and kissing you, according to the gossip sites. You didn't seem to object."

"Oh for— Argh! She's a lesbian! She doesn't even like men."

Not interested in his excuses, Hilary shook her head. "I'm not angry, and I don't blame you. You were free to be with whoever you wanted."

"Fine. I'm going to prove to you my feelings aren't going to change."

"Tricking me into having lunch with you isn't going to work."

His gaze was steady. "Just so you know, I'm not going to stop until I make my point."

"Do whatever you like. But I'm warning you back, I'm not easy to convince."

AFTER HILARY LEFT, MARK THREW EVERYTHING out. It was stupid to think he could convince her by doing something he wasn't comfortable with. Cooking. How ridiculous. He'd probably starve in a post-apocalyptic world because he didn't even know how to use a can opener.

Everyone thought his best friend Gavin was the one without any sense of proportion or common sense. When he and his wife Amandine had been going through some rough patches, he'd bought her a pink private jet and almost commissioned a yacht to be built. Well, wait until Mark unleashed everything in his power to convince Hilary he wasn't some fickle bastard like his father. She'd see what "out of proportion" *really* was.

He pulled out his mobile. He needed every weapon in his arsenal.

TWENTY-THREE

GAVIN DIDN'T SAY A WORD ABOUT THE lunch, and Hilary didn't either. She knew he had only been trying to help, and that he only knew Mark's side of the story. And that was the way it would stay; she wasn't going to give him her side. It was none of Gavin's business, just like his marital issues hadn't been any of hers.

And there had been no word from Mark since the lunch…as Hilary had privately predicted. A firm "no" and he'd moved on to try his luck with some other woman. Which was fine; she wished both of them well. She could move on, too.

Except that he'd said, "I love you."

Those three words circled in her head unrelentingly, but there was no way they could be true. He'd said them out of frustration—because she wouldn't give him another chance—or maybe it was something he said to all the women he dated.

Either way, she didn't want to think about it.

The rest of the week went as normal. No more surprise "go to my place to pick up something I forgot" tasks. Amandine hadn't hired an assistant yet, but Hilary was certain Kim would get the job. The young woman was smart, dedicated and well-organized—just the thing her boss's artist wife needed.

That Sunday Hilary finally moved into her new place. It was a fairly new apartment complex with great amenities. It wasn't even that far from the office, and the tenants were mostly young professionals, which was perfect. By the time the movers had set up her furniture and placed all the boxes where she wanted them, it was almost four. Hilary plopped on the floor and stretched out her legs. "Man, I'm going to be sore tomorrow."

"Tell me about it," Jo said, downing some kind of super mineral water with extra vitamins. She tossed one to Hilary. "Drink that. It should help."

Hilary looked at the cheery yellow label dubiously. "Does it really work?"

"Yup."

"No placebo effect?"

"I don't care what effect it is as long as it works."

Jo liked all natural healthy stuff, while Hilary preferred something that worked for certain and fast. Hilary took a small sip. The last "health" drink Jo had raved about had tasted like chemicals and dirt. This one had a hint of citrus, so Hilary downed it fast. She'd worked up a serious thirst.

Hilary's phone buzzed. Jo's eyes narrowed while Hilary checked the message. It was from Lila.

"Your aunt, right?" Jo said.

"Yeah."

"What does she want?"

"She said she has no appetite, but wanted to know if I planned to come by, in which case she'd make something."

"I swear, she just doesn't want to let you go."

"Guess not." Hilary sighed. It was really too bad about Lila, but it was obvious her aunt wanted drama in her life because it gave her the attention she craved. Lila needed to find a more positive force. Something like going out and getting herself a nice elderly gentleman friend who would treat her right. Hilary just couldn't be Lila's companion anymore. She needed to live her own life.

Jo went to the balcony and looked outside. "Maybe I should rent my place out and move here," she said. "Look at all those hot young male bodies by the pool. Mmm-hmm."

"Really?" Hilary didn't move from her spot. She had zero motivation. No man would ever compare to Mark. Maybe she'd be compelled to find some-body when time had put enough foggy layers over her memory so that her heart no longer ached at the thought of him. But right now, everything was too fresh and raw. She needed some time to grieve for the relationship that had been set up to fail from the beginning.

A clear male voice rose in a familiar melody from "Love Me Tender." More voices joined.

"Oh my god! Hilary, come on. Get up and come here." Urgency filled Jo's voice, and she waved her hand fast. "Now!"

That got Hilary to her feet. She went to stand next to Jo and watched six men by the pool sing a cappella. They started to move toward Hilary's unit. As the song reached its climax, they all held up their right index fingers, then made heart signs with their hands. Then each singer pulled out a card with a different letter on it. When they held them up in a row it spelled H-I-L-A-R-Y.

Was this what Mark had meant when he'd said he'd convince her of his love?

When it was finished, the spectators clapped. Her heart beat with something like scared little hope, and Hilary blinked away moisture gathering in her eyes before it could fall.

"Wow, that was great," Jo said.

"Yeah."

"So… Who's the mystery admirer?"

Hilary swallowed. "There's no mystery. It's Mark."

"Mark Pryce?" Jo's eyes grew large. "I thought you guys were finished."

"We are."

"I don't know." Jo said, folding her arms and sing-songing the last word. "It doesn't look finished."

"It's just a stunt. It doesn't mean anything," Hilary said, while her heart fluttered and chanted *liar, liar, liar.*

"You sure? It certainly looks like something."

The doorbell rang. Grateful for the interruption, Hilary went to answer it, only to be faced with a smiling delivery guy with a giant basket of pale pink orchids and a big box of Belgian chocolates. "Are you Ms. Hilary Rosenberg?"

"Yes."

"Please sign here."

She scrawled her name, feeling Jo's avid gaze on her back. As soon as the delivery guy left and the door closed, Jo pointed her perfectly manicured index finger at the flowers and chocolates. "See! The troubadours and now this!"

"Oh come on," Hilary said. "They're probably from Gavin. He knows I'm moving today."

"Really?" Jo snatched the card from the flower basket and read it. "I had no idea Gavin had a romantic interest in you."

"Gimme that!" Hilary took it from her best friend's hand. The message read: I love you. It wasn't signed, but she didn't need that to know who was responsible.

"He's crazy about you," Jo said. "I'm sure he's never told any of his exes 'I love you.' His sister said so."

"She must not know him that well. He's just unhappy about my ending the relationship early." *Liar, liar, liar.*

Hilary's phone buzzed. She looked at the text.

Hope you enjoyed the show. I love you.

She wasn't going to answer that. She wasn't.

How do you like the chocolate?

Definitely not going to dignify that either. She opened the package and shoved it at Jo. "Here you go."

"You don't want any?"

"I'm on a diet."

Jo snorted a laugh. "You? A *diet*? When pigs fly."

"Shut up."

The phone danced on the counter again. Ignoring it, Hilary crossed her arms and watched her friend enjoy a piece of dark chocolate.

"Ohmigod. It's eighty-five percent pure," Jo said, groaning loudly like she was about to orgasm. "You sure you don't want any?"

Eighty-five percent. Her favorite. It was no coincidence. Hilary closed her eyes, knowing she had lost.

She popped a piece into her mouth and moaned. "Oh my god."

"Mark knows his food."

Hilary nodded. Her phone buzzed again, and Jo put it in Hilary's hand. "Answer the damned thing. I don't think it's going to stop until you do."

"Fine." Hilary opened her eyes and flicked her finger over the screen.

I love you. Have dinner with me.

"What does it say?" Jo asked.

"It's a stalker."

Jo peered at her. "Is 'stalker' the new word for 'smokin' hot billionaire who's crazy about you'?"

"I told you, he's not crazy about me." Hilary had to remind herself of that critical fact before she did something stupid, like texting back *Okay*.

"He so is. Put him out of his misery. Go out with him. Have fun. Bebe's gone now, so you can't think he's doing this to do that whole half-sister-slash-cousin threesome thing you were worried about. You need some romance in your life, you know. And Walt doesn't count even if he did turn out to be innocent after all. You had zero chemistry with the guy. I'm not even sure why you thought to marry him."

Hilary ticked off the list of qualities she'd told herself trumped everything else. "Stable job. Good pay. Careful in his decisions. Well-educated."

Jo yawned. "Bo-ring. Where's the romance, Hilary? How about things like hottie, good in bed, well-hung, great body, nice ass, gorgeous mouth, amazing stamina, can make you wet with a look…" She leaned forward and lowered her voice. "You know…things that make life a little more interesting."

"That's how I ended up with Freddie. I wanted those things. The same with my mom and aunt and Tim. They wanted heat, passion and drama, and all of them ended up like that." Hilary rolled her wrist. "Mom lost the will to take care of herself once Tim was gone. So to get that amazing emotional high back, she started to self-medicate. When pot and E stopped working, she started on crack…and one day she OD'd. I am *not* going to be like her. I'm going to be a responsible person. An adult."

Jo sighed. "You are. That's the problem. You're too responsible. Imagine yourself in a nursing home thirty years from now. Are you going to look back and say, 'Wow, I had a great life. I was never late for work, and my vibrator worked pretty well.'"

Hilary tried to keep a serious look on her face, but ended up smiling. "It's not that simple."

"Nothing's ever simple. I just don't want you to ignore possibilities out of fear. Sometimes you have to take a leap of faith, believing that somebody's going to catch you."

Hilary made a noncommittal noise. Sure, for somebody like Jo—beautiful, successful, confident—it might be easier. But it wasn't so simple for Hilary. Mark wasn't just some fun guy who was good in bed. He had the power to destroy her, and she couldn't take that leap. What if, one day, he wasn't there to catch her?

AN HOUR LATER, MARK WAS ON THE PHONE. "So how did it go?"

"She liked it," Jo said. It had taken an hour to extricate herself from Hilary's place. "Although I think you should've serenaded her yourself."

"A man's got to know his limitations. I wanted her to enjoy it, not flee in horror."

She chuckled. "You did pretty well. I'm sort of impressed, but she's not totally into it yet."

"Well, I have other plans in the works."

"I wasn't kidding when I told you I'd kill you if you make her unhappy," Jo said.

"Don't worry. I wasn't kidding when I told you I'm going to make her the happiest woman in the world."

APPARENTLY HER LACK OF RESPONSE HADN'T deterred Mark at all. On Monday, every radio station in LA was playing songs dedicated to "the very special love of my life, Hilary Rosenberg" every hour on the hour. Hilary had to turn off the radio.

When she walked into the office, Sally jumped to her feet and said, "Oh my god, Hilary, it's so romantic."

Should she say it was a different Hilary Rosenberg? No. Sally would never believe it. Her name was too distinctive. Hilary shrugged. "Well. It's just some radio time. I'm sure they made a mistake."

"Not that, the a cappella. Totally cool!"

Hilary stared at Sally's enthused face. "How did you know abou—?"

"It's on YouTube! At the end of your song, they mentioned the impromptu a cappella from Sunday. So of course I had to check."

It seemed like every other person at the office gave her a thumbs up or wink as she walked past their desks. Okay, this was just weird. People didn't celebrate her choice of men or care this much about her romantic life.

Then she saw a giant bouquet of red and pink heart-shaped balloons tied to her chair. A basket of flowers had a message written in large block letters: I LOVE YOU. HAVE DINNER WITH ME.

"You totally should!" Sally said, bouncing left

and right. It was like she was the one who'd been asked out.

Hilary's phone vibrated. She checked the message. It was from Kim.

OMG Hilary, have you been listening to the radio? I had no idea you were the love of Mark's life!

Pete Monroe, an analyst at the firm and Gavin's brother-in-law, stopped by her desk. He was holding a big mug that read, "I can short an entire continent and still come out ahead." "Hey, Hilary. When's the happy occasion?"

"What happy occasion?" she almost snapped at him before she caught herself. It wasn't Pete's fault she was under siege.

"The wedding. Isn't that what Mark's gunning for?"

"Wedding?" she repeated, flabbergasted. She couldn't decide which would be preferable: spontaneously combusting or getting sucked down underground into one of the fiery pits of hell.

Pete blinked. "Why else would somebody like him go through all this trouble?"

"There's no wedding. None. Absolutely *none.*"

"Okay." He shrugged and returned to his office.

Sally watched him go, then turned to Hilary. "Are you sure? You can tell me."

"Sally, seriously. No. There's nothing. You watch—it's going to end soon enough." Mark would grow bored when he kept getting ignored. He wasn't used to that.

"Really?" The other woman's face crumbled a bit. "What a shame. Still…" She sighed. "I'd love to experience something like this at least once. It's just so…grand."

By the time four o'clock rolled around, Hilary absolutely despised the word "grand." Everyone from her coworkers to friends to strangers had decided to call her "love life" *grand*. At least Mark hadn't plastered her face all over the Internet and TV. That allowed her to walk around the city without other people sighing "Grand Romance" at her.

She could handle this. Later that day, she was flying to New York City with Gavin and his wife on an overnight business trip. Mark wasn't going to chase her all the way to the other end of the country.

Gavin took his plane on the trip, instead of the pink jet he'd bought for his wife. Amandine sat next to him while holding their baby boy, and she looked at Hilary. "I always knew one day Mark would find the woman of his dreams, and I'm so happy it's you."

Hilary forced a smile, hoping none of her annoyance came through. "Oh I don't know. Given his reputation, I'm sure he's going to stop once he realizes I'm not interested."

"You think so? But still… A cappella? All the radio stations in the city playing songs to you? It's incredibly romantic."

Gavin snorted. "Private jets and yachts are just as romantic—and more practical."

Amandine laughed. "I'm not saying what you did wasn't, but this is just so sweet. Like a fairytale."

And it was. That was the problem. Mark was supposed to be a shallow and self-centered playboy who got bored easily. And Hilary was supposed to be a hard-nosed career woman whose heart didn't bend one bit at the sight of the happy couple before her. They seemed so open and loving...Hilary ached for something like that for herself, but knew it would never happen. They hadn't had the kind of screwed up life she had. They didn't have the taint of the Rosenberg blood.

In her hotel room, she dropped her bag and sighed heavily. As usual, her room was beautifully appointed and furnished. Gavin didn't believe in traveling cheap. Normally she would enjoy the trip. It was nice to leave L.A. once in a while and spend a night or two in a five-star hotel with impeccable service.

After her evening rituals, she lay in bed, staring at the ceiling. *Midnight*, she thought. *And I'm alone.*

Mark had been charming over the past few days, but he wasn't Prince Charming...and she wasn't Cinderella. And somehow tears started to flow as she realized there was too great a distance separating them.

TWENTY-FOUR

THERE WAS NO A CAPPELLA OR FLOWERS OR chocolates or balloons the next morning. Hilary took a long breath. She was relieved—no, happy—that Mark wasn't trying any more over-the-top antics. It was taking a little longer than she'd thought, but he seemed to be losing interest.

So why did her heart feel funny, like there was a hollow spot in the center of it, if this was what she'd wanted?

Gavin had some meetings in Manhattan, and Amandine decided she wanted to go to The Museum of Modern Art. After breakfast, the three of them left the hotel together.

"God, it looks even bigger in daylight," Amandine said.

"You've never been to New York City?" Hilary said, surprised that her cosmopolitan boss's wife seemed so awed by the city.

"I never had the chance. It's amazing how everything's so flashy and busy all the time. It's not like L.A. with its Hollywood glamour, but it has its own charm." Amandine looked up. "I especially like the way they use the sides of the buildings as ad displays everywhere. There's nothing like that in…" She trailed off.

"What?" Gavin said.

"Is that…? Oh my *god*."

Hilary's head snapped up. Five enormous LED screens, sitting high on adjacent skyscrapers, read: *I'll love you forever, Hilary*. Taken together, the signs dwarfed everything else on the skyline.

"Wow," Gavin and Amandine said at the same time, then looked at her.

Hilary felt her cheeks heat. Her heart thumped like crazy. This was a pretty serious declaration. It wasn't something he could deny later, or pretend was some kind of misunderstanding. How could he change his mind after this?

She shook herself mentally. People routinely spent money to declare their love and commitment to each other all the time in front of witnesses. But they still ended up in divorce court as often as not. Her boss had been pretty close to that himself. This kind of public display couldn't possibly measure up…even if people *were* staring at the display and taking pictures with their phones.

What if this is real though? Would she be okay with letting Mark go?

She clutched her purse and briefcase to her chest, her eyes glued to the display.

I'll love you forever, Hilary.

She wanted to believe it so bad, the pain was almost physical.

THE NEXT DAY, GAVIN'S JET FLEW TOWARD A SMALL private airport on the outskirts of L.A. It was only three o'clock on the west coast, thanks to the time difference. Hilary proofread the meeting minutes and a few other documents, while her boss and his wife dozed. They'd been out late the night before, enjoying the city. Hilary saved all the files and shut down her laptop with a sigh. Her heart still beat a bit too fast, and every time she thought of Mark's big gesture in New York City, her face grew hot. She pressed a glass of iced water to her cheeks.

I love you. Have dinner with me.

That was all that Mark had sent in private, while making his—dammit, there was no other word— grand declaration in public. She couldn't imagine what he might want to say to her over dinner. "I love you" was the most obvious choice, but he'd already said that. None of her exes had been this persistent or over-the-top, so she was in new territory. Gavin was pretty over-the-top too, but he was more into buying outrageous presents than gestures that would get people's tongues wagging. The New York display incident was already all over the net, and the office had probably started a betting pool on what Mark would do next. That was just how Gavin's traders would amuse themselves while working ungodly numbers of hours each day.

They landed and deplaned, Gavin starting down the stairs first, Amandine and Hilary following. Suddenly, Amandine stopped dead and gasped.

"What is it?" Hilary said from behind her. Still inside the aircraft, she couldn't see much outside since the other woman was blocking her view at the door, but she could hear the drone of plane engines…*above them?*

"Hilary… Look." Amandine stood aside and Hilary stepped out and looked up.

Planes were flying intricate patterns in the clear Los Angeles sky. Colored smoke plumed out of their ends, and they created a giant pink heart with an arrow through it. Blood roared in Hilary's head, and she felt like her own heart would explode…like she'd run a hundred miles.

Then the smoke changed to white, and they wrote: *Mark and Hilary 4EVER.*

The message should've seemed juvenile. High schoolish, really. Except it made her eyes fill with tears, and she couldn't stop them from spilling over her cheeks. Nobody had ever thought she was worth this much effort. A Rosenberg girl was somebody a guy slept with, maybe had wild sex with…but not somebody he cooked for, arranged a cappella for, dedicated songs to, rented out Manhattan LED screens for, or hired a team of pilots for a fancy air show for.

"Oh, Hilary." Amandine's expression crumbled when she took one look at Hilary. Did she look that bad?

Amandine turned to Gavin. "Why don't you wait for us in the car?" Then she wrapped an arm around Hilary's shoulder. "What's wrong? I thought you'd be happy."

"I am, but I'm so scared. I feel like this isn't real. It just can't be happening to me," Hilary blurted out, unable to contain it.

"It's very real, and you should believe it." Amandine handed her a handkerchief. "Mark is crazy about you."

"But for how long?" Hilary wiped her tears and sniffled.

"You'll never find out unless you give him a chance, will you?" Amandine searched Hilary's face. "It's normal to be scared, Hilary. You remember when Gavin and I were going through that… rough phase? I was scared too when he wouldn't let me go. I was so sure I'd fall even more deeply in love with him only to lose him in the end."

"How could you ever think that? He adores you."

"I know that now, but back then I didn't. I wasn't certain I was good enough for him."

Fresh tears welled in Hilary's eyes. "I *know* I'm not good enough."

"Mark's no dummy. If you really weren't worth it, he wouldn't go through all this trouble. You're a great woman, Hilary. You just don't realize it, which only makes you that much sweeter." Amandine gave her a tight hug. "Do what feels right to you and what will make you happy." She pulled back and gave Hilary a quick grin. "You drove here, right? Why don't you take the rest of the day off?"

"But Gavin ne—"

"Gavin won't mind." Amandine gave her a wink. "I'll make sure of it."

Hilary tilted her head back and looked at the fluffy messages in the perfect blue sky.

Heart.

Mark and Hilary 4EVER.

Her heart thumped.

She was at the precipice.

Jump. Jump. Jump.

If she got this close and stepped back, she'd regret it for the rest of her life. Jo was right. When she was old and on her last legs, Hilary didn't want to think about what could've been. She wanted to be able to talk to her grandchildren about the great romance of her life. About how much Mark loved her.

She pulled out her phone and scrolled down until she found his last text. *I love you. Have dinner with me.*

Her hands shaking, she typed: *Okay.*

"So how does she look?" Mark asked, pacing. At the rate things were going, he'd need to replace the damned carpet in his home office.

"Crying," Gavin said.

Mark wanted to bang his head against his desk. "What *kind* of crying? Good crying or bad crying?"

"I don't know. Amandine's with her right now. She just gave Hilary a big hug. I'm not sure if that's good or bad."

"You're so useless." He should've never asked Gavin, whose obtuseness concerning women would make a pile of bricks appear positively romantic by comparison. Mark should've hired a private detective—a female one—to watch Hilary instead and report on her reactions.

"Hey, give me a break. I never have to figure out my employees' moods. It's their job to figure out mine."

"You know what? After she marries me, I'm going to make sure she quits."

"What?! You can't do that."

"Sure, I can. I'm not saying she can't work. She just can't work for you."

"Don't be a hater. Oh wait. Amandine's coming in."

"Thank god. Lemme talk to her. I'm sure she can tell me better than you."

"There's a small possibility that you might potentially be right. Hold on."

A moment later Amandine was on the line. "Hey, Mark. That was some show there."

"Thanks. Was Hilary impressed?"

"Well, yes, but…"

His stomach twisted at the way she hesitated. "What?"

"I don't know if you're on the right track. You're making these grand gestures, and I admit they're very impressive. But romance means intimacy. You might consider doing things face-to-face so she can look into your eyes and see the truth in them. Does that make sense?"

"Totally. The thing is, I tried that and it didn't work. She's convinced I'm going to be like my dad." And it hurt him that he had nothing to counter her belief. His reputation was pretty crappy when it came to women. If he'd known this day would come, he would've been more careful and circumspect.

"Well, why don't you try again? She might surprise you."

But Hilary wouldn't even have dinner with him. He was keenly aware of the lack of response from her. How in the hell was he supposed to look into her eyes and be all sincere and romantic when she wouldn't even answer his texts?

Then his phone buzzed. He glanced at it. Hilary. "Gotta go," he said, pressing it to his ear again. "I'll call you later." He hung up and checked the message.

Okay.

He blinked. Then his mouth dried and he felt light-headed. Shit. She'd said yes to dinner.

But was it a good yes or a bad yes? Then he almost smacked himself for even thinking that. There was no such thing as a bad yes.

He looked around his penthouse, realizing that he needed the maid service again, and quick. A blanket was on the floor in front of the TV—he still wasn't able to sleep in his own bed—and a soggy pizza box lay on the coffee table. An old shirt and shorts covered his couch. Nothing had been wiped down in the last seven days, and the kitchen sink was full of dirty plates and bowls. He cursed. There was less than four hours to get everything ready. He was having dinner later that day, and not giving her an opportunity to change her mind. No way.

This time, nothing would be left to chance.

He wrote: *I'll pick you up at seven at your place. See you then.*

The dinner would be the ultimate test. He'd have to tell her everything in his heart, so she knew this was the real deal, not some temporary infatuation. Mark Pryce did not do temporary infatuation with the love of his life. He'd freaking jump out of an airplane before letting her shed another tear because of him.

He took a deep breath. He could do this. He so freaking could.

TWENTY-FIVE

J O SHOWED UP AT FIVE SHARP, HAULING SEVEN giant bags of dresses and shoes. "I did the best I could given how little time I had to work with."

"Thank you so much," Hilary said.

"I'm sure the boutique owners thought I was dressing somebody to meet the President or something."

Hilary laughed. "Did they?"

"Look at all this." Jo hefted the bags, then squinted at Hilary. "God, your makeup's a mess."

"I know. I tried to fix it, but I keep crying."

"Honey, the man loves you. Stop crying and start thinking about all the dirty things you can do with him."

Hilary flushed.

"I can't believe it. You're blushing like a sixteen year-old virgin or something!" Jo dumped everything on the bed. "I couldn't get anything in ivory, which is a shame since it looks so good on you, but we'll just have to deal. How about this lavender one?" She pulled up a shimmery silk cocktail dress. "The cut is stunning and really shows off your curves. Or we could go more traditional and do something black, but I don't know about that color and you today."

"Lavender," Hilary said. There was nothing traditional about the way her relationship with Mark had progressed.

"Great choice."

Almost two hours of fussing and styling later, Jo declared Hilary was ready for the showdown. "You're going to knock him dead."

"You think so?"

"Girl, you look scorching hot. Mark's going to fall to his knees and kiss your feet."

"Thank you," Hilary said, with real feeling. The dress clung to all the right places, emphasizing her hourglass figure. The diamond drop earrings and necklace completed what she thought of as a classy siren look, and she knew she would've never been able to put it together this quickly without Jo's help.

Jo gave her a tight hug. "Happy to help out, Hilary. Now go knock him dead."

When Hilary went out to the limo, a sharp stab of disappointment hit her at the empty interior. "Where's Mark?" she asked the uniformed driver.

"I'm sorry, Ms. Rosenberg. He's waiting for you at his home," he said in a soft voice. "Shall we go?"

"Uh…yeah. Sure," she said. She'd been so certain Mark would pick her up.

The driver opened the door for her and she slid inside. As the limo pulled out from her place, her palms grew slick.

She took several deep breaths. *This is going to be okay. No matter how things turn out, I'll be fine.* She told herself this over and over so she didn't bolt from sheer panic.

MARK CHECKED EVERYTHING A FINAL TIME. IT WAS all perfect, exactly the way he wanted. His insides were churning the way they always did right before he opened a new restaurant. Except this was an even more important event.

His penthouse was spotless, thanks to the emergency housekeeping service. Two hundred and fifty orchids had been brought in and the dining area smelled of fresh flowers and exquisite French cuisine.

The driver called. "I have Ms. Rosenberg."

"Good." Mark placed both hands on the counter and closed his eyes, head bowed. Taking a moment. He hadn't been sure if she would come until the call.

She could've always changed her mind, and there would have been nothing he could do about it.

A few minutes later the driver called again to let him know Hilary was on her way up. Quickly, he finished setting the table. André had done a great job with dinner. He'd been determined to save Mark's "doomed love affair," after hearing about the "grand failure" of lunch at Gavin's home.

The bell rang. Mark cleared his throat before opening it…and there she stood looking like a vision in a dress that shimmered like mother of pearl.

"Hey," she said, her face unreadable.

"Hi. Come on in." His hands flexed with the need to touch her, but he controlled himself. He hadn't waited this long to screw things up now.

"I thought we were going to a restaurant," she murmured, taking in the flowers.

"We are. It's a new one called Chez Mark."

"Ah."

"No, I considered it, but decided this was better. More private."

She turned and looked at him. A smile ghosted on her lips. "What on earth could you tell me in private that you haven't said all over the country already?"

The question threw him. He'd had everything all planned out. They'd wine and dine, chat a bit.

He'd tell her how much he loved her again, this time with all the damn eye contact she could handle, so she'd know how serious and sincere he was. Then he'd go on bended knee and propose.

Except all those things sort of vanished from his mind. He didn't want to eat—couldn't, not when he had no idea if she was going to have faith in him and his love. He wished he could pull his heart out of his chest and show it to her...but he couldn't. So he opted for Plan B.

He pulled out a velvet jewelry box and hesitated. He knew a lot of great moves, but he had no idea what to do in a moment like this. Before he could lose courage, he thrust it at her, his fingers tight around the box so they wouldn't shake. "This."

The smile vanished, and she pulled her lips in even as her eyes got wide. Finally she said, "Mark... This... I thought this was just dinner." She blinked away tears. "This isn't some...game of escalation. You're just starting to tell me you love me and now..."

He took her hand, willing her to feel what he felt. "Do you think it's a game to me? I bared my heart and soul to you in front of the entire country. Do you think I'd do that for a woman I was planning to ditch in three months?"

A tear slid down her cheek.

"I'm going to keep at it until you tell me to my face that you don't want me...or else you finally realize I mean it when I say I love you and want to spend the rest of my life with you. I can't change my upbringing or my past. But I can change my future. I'll spend the rest of my life loving you the way you deserve to be loved." He dropped to one knee and opened the box, showing her a pink princess-cut diamond ring. It had reminded him of her and what they could have together. "Hilary… Will you take a chance on me?"

HILARY COULDN'T STOP THE TEARS. HOW CRAZY when she'd thought she was cried out already.

And she wanted to speak but she couldn't push the words out through the big lump in her throat. So she did the second best thing she could and launched herself at him, dropping to her knees, wrapping her arms around his neck and pulling him down for a long, deep kiss.

His strong hands settled on her back and pulled her close. He tasted like the brightest possible future, the future she was always afraid would never be hers because she was a Rosenberg. She wanted to be in his arms forever, kissing him like this forever, but she knew he deserved a real answer. She broke the kiss briefly and whispered, "Yes" against his lips.

"I thought you'd never say that," he said, his voice shaky and thick.

"I was afraid, Mark. I thought maybe you'd wake up and wonder what the heck you were doing with somebody like me, when you could have anybody in the world."

"Crazy, crazy woman." He pressed his forehead against hers, then took a deep breath and put the ring on her finger. It looked perfect, just like their love. "I should spank you for making me as crazy as you are."

She gave him a small smile, but there was a gleam in her eye as well. "Is that so?"

"Well… I guess now I can call off the space shuttle."

"*Space shuttle?*"

"I was going to launch one…have them fly it in geosynchronous orbit over the city. It was going to be called the *Marry Me Hilary.*"

"I haven't driven you crazy. You were crazy from the beginning," she said with a laugh.

"Desperate times call for desperate measures, and all that. If announcing my love for you to the world wasn't enough, I had no choice but to do it to the solar system."

She put her hands on his cheeks and cradled his face. She'd never told any man this, and she wanted him to know she meant every word. "I love you, Mark. I'm the luckiest woman in the entire universe."

His gorgeous face split into a radiant smile.

"And I'm the luckiest man in the universe. What a perfect pair we make."

"So…about that dinner…"

"Yes?"

"Think it can wait?" she murmured, gently pulling at his lower lip with her teeth.

His answer was a soul-searing kiss.

THANK YOU FOR READING *THE BILLIONAIRE'S Counterfeit Girlfriend.* I hope you enjoyed it!

Would you like to know when my next book is available? Send a blank message to new-from-nadia@aweber.com or go to my website at www.nadialee.net to sign up for my new release alert.

Coming up next is *Merry in Love* (Meredith Lloyd & Daniel Aylster). Look for it this winter! (Or—just like above—send a blank message to new-from-nadia@aweber.com or go to my website at www.nadialee.net to sign up for my new release mailing list!)

Reviews and ratings help other readers find books. I'd really appreciate it if you can take a moment to review and/or rate this book!

I love to hear from readers! Feel free to write me at nadia@nadialee.net or follow me on Twitter @nadialee, or like my Facebook page at www.facebook.com/nadialeewrites or join my reader group at http://www.nadialee.net/fb-group. Say hello and let me know which one of my characters is your favorite or what you want to see next or anything else you want to talk about! I personally read all my emails, Tweets and Facebook comments.

WHAT'S NEXT?

Coming up next is *Merry in Love* (Daniel Aylster & Meredith Lloyd). If you want to know when it's out, send a blank message to new-from-nadia@aweber.com or go to my website at www.nadialee.net to sign up for my new release alert!

ABOUT NADIA LEE

NEW YORK TIMES AND USA TODAY BESTSELLING author Nadia Lee writes sexy, emotional contemporary romance. Born with a love for excellent food, travel and adventure, she has lived in four different countries, kissed stingrays, been bitten by a shark, ridden an elephant and petted tigers.

Currently, she shares a condo overlooking a small river and sakura trees in Japan with her husband and son. When she's not writing, she can be found reading books by her favorite authors or planning another trip.

To learn more about Nadia and her projects, please visit www.nadialee.net. To receive updates about upcoming works from Nadia, please visit www.nadialee.net to subscribe to her new release alert.

CPSIA information can be obtained
at www.ICGtesting.com
Printed in the USA
BVOW09s0901080418
512775BV00001B/51/P